THE CRYSTAL QUEST

ADDISON HEFFERNAN

Paperback ISBN: 978-1-63616-201-0
eBook ISBN: 978-1-63616-206-5

Published By Opportune Independent Publishing Co.
www. opportunepublishing.com

Printed in the United States of America

For permission requests, please email the publisher with the subject line as "Attention: Permissions Coordinator"
to the email address below:

Info@Opportunepublishing.com

For Mom and Dad
Love you both to the moon and back

TABLE OF CONTENTS

CHAPTER ONE

Dani Stallard hated dungeons.

They were dark, creepy, and very, very old.

Naturally, her twin brother, Will, was obsessed with them—the one under their palace, more specifically.

"Why are we down here again?" she asked, her long gown nearly making her trip.

She'd nearly been in Breckindale for a year and she'd only visited the dungeon once. Dani avoided it if she could.

"Because we turn fourteen in a month and a half! Don't you think we should be trying to cram in as many adventures as possible?"

Dani sighed. "Sure, but we have tons of secret passageways to do that in. Why here?"

At that, Will gave his most innocent smile. "Because you don't like it." He shrugged.

"Cruel," Dani observed. "So, what are we looking for anyway?"

The faster the treasure hunt ended, the faster she could leave.

"Old stuff," Will said. "Anything left down here from prisoners."

"Has anyone ever told you that you're insane?"

"Just you, constantly."

Dani raised an eyebrow in challenge.

"Okay, and Libby."

Dani shot a sympathetic smile in his direction. "Poor you. Being told off by your sister and her bodyguard."

"Whatever. I'm going to go explore now, and just for saying that, you're going to come with me."

Will grabbed her arm, pulling her forward. Dani sighed but didn't argue. She did, however, wish that she'd insisted at least one of her guards came with her.

"First, we should check out that weird room you found. Remember that?"

How could she not? The year prior, a scroll had been addressed to Dani from a secret society that she now knew was called The Golden Eagle. Giselle, one of the royal advisors, had snuck it to her in secret, and after Will had snooped around her room, Dani had been forced to hide it in the dungeon. In doing so, she'd stumbled upon a hidden room with a box, medallion, and note inside belonging to Delacour.

The medallion made a lot more sense now that Dani understood the organization it was from.

"It's still here."

Dani stared at the chest, still where she'd left it during her previous visit. "Did Mom and Dad ever figure out what this room actually was?” she asked her brother.

Will shook his head. “Dad thought it was a war room of some kind.”

“Huh.”

Dani had figured it was some sort of secret meeting room of sorts, at least originally. It was similar to the inside of the main base of Frovland: Blitzspire.

“It’s pretty cool that we have a secret room in our dungeon,” Will considered, always at his happiest exploring.

“Almost as cool as the turret in Greenaway?” Dani asked.

Greenaway House was the large estate that the Varrons lived in, not far from Umbergrove where the Callisto family lived. Amery and Lydia didn’t agree on much, but they both loved the turret just as much as Dani did now.

Will considered for a second before answering. “I would say that we win.”

“Sure,” Dani teased.

Will frowned. “You’re just grumpy!”

“Grumpy?” Dani cracked a grin.

One of her biggest joys in life was annoying her twin brother.

“I’m going to go see if I can find anything in the cells. Do you want to come?”

“Do you think I’d want to come?”

Will snorted. "No, but I would never leave you out of a Stallard Twin Adventure."

"Go explore. I'll be here," Dani told him, already waving him off.

Will hurried away, excitement playing across his features as Dani opened up the box and stared at its contents.

The medallion wasn't anything special—at least in comparison to the one Dani kept carefully hidden. It was gold like hers, engraved like hers, and was embedded with an identical sliver of frost crystal that could blink to Frovland.

The other object inside was a handwritten note that Dani had forgotten even existed until she unfurled it in her hand and read it aloud.

"Never fall if you can spare a jump."

Dani was sure that the words were from Delacour, some sort of encouragement or advice or secret code that was left unsolved by her predecessor before her death.

It was hard to tell which.

Delacour had been the original chosen one. She'd saved the entire realm at thirteen and brought it out of the dark age by defeating a group called the Order of the Raven with her sparks. After she'd named herself a Sparker and made history, Delacour had decided to form The Golden Eagle because a prophecy told her that one day, her heir would be put in the same position and suffer the same fate that Delacour had been warned about.

Dani became its leader after the Winter Ball during her first week in the realm. She had help, of course, from her Sparker instructor Sir Hugo and the rest of her golden-clad council, but the position weighed heavily on her at times. Especially when she remembered the downsides.

She wasn't allowed to tell anyone about The Golden Eagle. That meant lying to her dad, brother, friends, and everyone else who had questions about what had actually happened in Frovland.

Libby had been the one to come up with the excuse of the secret society having known Delacour in the past and wanting to offer Dani some advice passed down from her ancestor. That had been it.

A lie was only a lie if she didn't mean it, and when Will asked about it shortly after Dani had returned, completely shaken after finding out that her mother was actually a member of the organization, she made sure to believe it as much as she could.

No one but Anders, Libby, and Amandine knew that she blinked to Frovland nearly every night for training sessions and war meetings with her council.

That was how it had to be. Even if it made Dani so frustrated that she wanted to scream.

She put the paper down and closed the box with a satisfying thud. Thinking too hard about her complicated duties wouldn't make any difference, and Dani knew it. She'd reminded herself of it over and over and over.

"Not to be a bummer, but you and Will need to change. The luncheon starts in less than an hour, and guests will be arriving in half that."

Libby peeked her head in, her blonde and pink streaked hair in a side ponytail.

Technically, neither Stallard was supposed to be in the dungeon or exploring or doing anything but preparing for the nobility luncheon their parents were hosting.

Will followed rules to an extent. Dani followed rules all the way through.

As far as their parents and butler, Grantham, knew, the two of them were doing homework in Will's room. Their heads of security, Anders and Leo, hadn't argued that much when they'd snuck off to the dungeon, but they did promise to stand guard.

"Got it."

Dani followed her out, leaving behind the box and finding her brother exiting the direction of the old cells. "Come on, Mom and Dad will be mad if we're late. Even more so if they find out why."

Her brother frowned. "Why do you always have to be the responsible one?"

"Because you're not." Dani grinned, mostly because getting ready was genuinely going to take her a while.

"Girls," Will grumbled.

Dani rolled her eyes, but a smile turned up her lips anyway. She and Will had gotten close in the months she'd been in Breckindale, and even though it wasn't enough to make up for the thirteen years they'd been apart, their relationship was normal by twin standards. They bickered, they teased, they protected each other.

Sometimes, it was enough to keep Dani from thinking about the lies that she'd told him about Frovland. The things that she was keeping from him.

Still, that wasn't by choice.

It also wasn't her fault.

"How many people are attending this one?" Dani asked Anders once she made it out of the dungeon with Libby behind her.

Her head of security gave her a sharp look. "I'm not telling you that information."

Dani sighed. "Oh, come on. I want to know."

"Forgive me, have we not had this discussion before?"

Dani may have gained plenty of experience and training from her etiquette lessons, but she still got nervous at any royal event she was forced to attend. Especially when she found out the amount of people that would be there.

Anders noticed everything, and when he noticed that months ago, he stopped answering any of her questions.

She turned to Libby at the same time Will exited the dungeon and closed its heavy door.

"Don't look at me! I've been sworn to secrecy too!" Libby threw up her hands.

"It's just nobility," Will answered when she switched her gaze again.

He looked perfectly calm, but he'd also been doing these things practically his whole life.

"Is Grandma coming, at least?" Dani hung back to walk in step with her brother.

"According to Mom, it's just the four of us," Will answered. "And the Magicals, apparently."

The Magicals were an elite council of brytlyns who helped the King and Queen govern. Dani liked the majority of them, a few she knew well, and there was one whom she seemed to be in a feud with.

"Makes sense," Dani agreed.

If the only royals in attendance were going to be them and their parents, then the Magicals would definitely be needed.

"This means that you'll have to be civil," Libby told her, like a big sister scolding her mischievous younger sibling.

"I'm always civil," Dani promised.

Libby raised a brow. "Last time, you hid behind Anders when Iris walked by so she didn't see you."

"She was glaring at me from across the room," Dani defended.

"That's true!" Will agreed.

Libby sighed. "Believe me, I don't like Iris any more than you do, but you can't pull that again."

Dani crossed her arms over her chest. "The day before, she told Mom and Dad that I was embarrassing the monarchy by not scoring high enough on my finals."

Anders turned back. "If she threatens you—"

"You'll handle it. I know." Dani had heard the phrase at least two dozen times since she'd been introduced to her bodyguard. For a former lieutenant in the royal military, Anders took his job protecting a teenager very seriously.

"I won't hide this time," she promised Libby, "but I'm making no promises about glaring if she starts it."

Months ago, Dani wouldn't have even considered starting a glare war with a high councilor. A lot had changed since her move, including her.

She wasn't the wide-eyed and completely terrified girl she'd been finding out that magic existed. Now, she was the Savior, the leader of a secret organization, and, most importantly, a princess who was most definitely going to be late for a party.

CHAPTER TWO

Dani made it outside the ballroom just in time to stand with her brother before the doors opened and the family was supposed to walk in and greet all of their guests.

"Grantham is going to have your head," Will informed her as they followed Callan and Amandine in. The Magicals were already working the room.

"I figured." Dani had noticed their rule stickler butler narrowing his eyes at her since she'd arrived. "How did you get down here so fast?"

"I had my clothes out and didn't take forever doing my hair."

"I don't take forever." Dani frowned. "And Libby did it." She reached up to touch the small braid that was woven through the front part of her hair.

"She's multi-talented," Will relented.

"Usually, Mom does it, but I was in a rush and she was already downstairs."

"And if you had made it downstairs ten minutes ago, you would have been greeted by the Magicals, and Iris already noticed your absence," Will added.

"Oh, good." Dani wondered if her smile looked as fake as she meant it. "Anders, do you see her anywhere?"

She'd promised Libby no hiding, but she never said anything about running away.
"She's with Cordelia and Ronan on the other side of the room."

The look he gave her clearly meant he saw right through her question, but in true Anders fashion, he didn't scold her for it.

"Lovely," Dani said. "We can stay and chat on this side."

"I'm not sure I'm liking this newfound confidence of yours." Anders looked too much like a tired dad for Dani not to crack a smile.

"Me neither, but she's lethal when she gets angry, so I just try to stay on her good side," Will advised, moving his arm a split second before Dani pinched him. "My point exactly!"

"I'm sorry. I get antsy when I'm tired," Dani belatedly apologized. "Nightmares?" Will's cheerful demeanor grew serious.

She nodded, blinking her shadowed eyes.
"The usual one."

Dani had been having nightmares since finding the prophecy. They usually revolved around her final battle and ended with her death right before she'd wake up in a cold sweat.

Sometimes, she was alone when it happened.
The worst ones included a loved one or friend getting killed first.

Will frowned. "You can come get me any time."

"I know."

Her brother's bedroom was right next to hers, and after a particularly hard nightmare resulting in their parents calling the royal physician, Will had promised that she could wake him up any time they got too bad.

Dani loved her brother more than anything, but he could read minds, and even though he wasn't supposed to, he read hers when he got worried.

She smiled, not wanting to think of the prophecy any more than she already had to. "Don't worry; I'm fine. Aren't we supposed to be socializing?"

"Yep, and Grantham sees us, so I should definitely get on that." Will gave him a wave and then hurried off to the opposite side of the ballroom. "You're still going to help me through this, right?" Dani asked Anders.

"I'll make the introductions," Anders promised.

"Thank you," Dani said gratefully.

Her etiquette lessons had taught her a lot about being a princess, and her confidence had grown, but small talk still freaked her out.

Libby's job was to step in if Dani needed help and to make sure that she didn't make a fool of herself.

"Your Highness, the Countess of Halsworth."

"Thank you for coming," Dani greeted, just as she'd been taught to do. "Have you been enjoying the luncheon?"

"It's been very lov—"

"Pardon me. I was told to collect the princess."

Dani knew that voice. Any other time, Anders would step in, but this time, he didn't even move.

"Excuse me." Dani offered a polite smile and then turned back to see a pair of blond twins grinning. Before she could say anything, they were pulling her through the crowd. "I didn't know you guys were coming!"

Amery Varron's hair was perfectly combed, and his jerkin and pants were perfectly pressed, but he looked just as mischievous and full of energy as usual. "It's a luncheon for nobility, Mystery. Of course we came."

"You didn't mention it at lunch on Friday," Dani reminded him, pointedly ignoring the nickname.

"We didn't know that we were coming until last night," Lydia admitted, crossing her arms over her purple gown.

Dani had noticed a few brytlyns her age in the ballroom, but she hadn't realized that her friends might possibly be in attendance too.

"Are Everett and Eldridge here too?"

"They went to save Will, I think." Amery shrugged.

"Where are we going?"

"Come on, Mystery, this isn't your first time at a luncheon."

"The dessert table?" Dani guessed.

"Bingo!" Amery cheered.

Dani glowered. "If you steal the fudge cakes again, we're having a repeat of The Great Fudge Ban."

"You mean when we all realized that my best friend is an evil genius?" Lydia checked.

Amery shook his head so hard his perfectly gelled hair moved. "No! No! No! Don't give her praise for it. I got sweets stolen for almost two weeks. It was torture!"

"You survived," Lydia reminded him.

"Barely, Lyds. Barely."

"Don't steal my fudge cakes and you'll be fine," Dani promised, and she could've sworn Anders cracked a smile.

"Yes, ma'am." Amery gave a salute right as they made it to the long table.

"I take it that you were ambushed too?" Will asked, already waiting alongside Everett and Eldridge.

"It was very convenient," Dani agreed, taking a plate.

"You're both very welcome," Everett told them.

"Thank you," Dani said.

"I planned this!" Amery held a hand up.

"Thank you," Will told him.

Amery put a hand on his heart. "You're very welcome, Freddie."

"Freddie?" Eldridge snorted.

"I'm trying out some new nickname ideas. Will got old years ago."

Sometimes, Dani forgot that her brother's full name was Wilfred. Their parents really liked giving long first names to their twins, and both of them despised them. If Amery had tried to call her Elle, Dani probably would have had the same reaction that Will did: slugging him in the shoulder after making sure no one was looking.

Amery gave his best dramatic sigh. "I'll keep working on it, I suppose."

Dani had never expected to have friends. She'd made it her whole life without any and survived being invisible for years. Now, she was in the center of a friend group full of noble pranksters and the best friend of one of the smartest brytlyns in school.

Her conscience liked to remind her that she could lose them. It wasn't a lie, but it was terrifying nonetheless. They knew that she was a Sparker and that she was the Savior, but they had no clue that she was the leader of a secret organization.

Sir Hugo had been insistent that telling them about The Golden Eagle compromised its ability to protect her, and Dani had been debating with him about it for months.

No progress had been made, and Dani was scared that if her friends found out the secrets that she'd been keeping, they'd ditch her.

"Hey, are you okay?" Lydia nudged her, breaking the hold paranoia had on Dani.

Dani nodded, forcing herself to focus on the dizzying party. "Yeah, I'm fine."

"Are you sure?" Lydia's voice softened.

Dani promised that she was, but Anders led her to a corner anyway, and she saw him signal to Libby from across the room.

"What's going on?" And then she felt it. The familiar lurch in her stomach and warmth in her fingers.

Sir Hugo had been working on her control constantly since their first session, and she had greatly improved her ability to suppress her emotions enough to not trigger her power.

Her hands were glowing. A sight that she'd seen many, many times but had only sent a shockwave of fear through her body once before.

Manifesting as a Sparker had been terrifying. Dani had only gotten over her fear of the power by getting a prophecy that predicted her death.

This time didn't make her as fearful, but it was much more unsettling.

Her hands were glowing. But they were glowing white.

CHAPTER THREE

"What does that mean?" Will asked.

"I don't know," Dani replied, her eyes fixed on her glowing hands.

"Have you ever shone white before?" Libby already knew the answer. She demanded it like she didn't.

"Never." Dani had only ever seen her hands glow red, the same color as her sparks.

"Why don't we get some air," Anders suggested, scanning the room again in two seconds flat.

Dani knew that he just wanted her out of the room just in case she lost control. The majority of Breckindale still didn't know what her power was, and this was not the way to share it.

"Good idea," Will agreed, any hints of humor on his face long gone.

"What can we do?" Eldridge asked.

Dani didn't want them to worry. It would make her worry more. "Stay here. I'm fine; don't worry."

But was she?

The moment before, she'd felt perfectly normal, but now she felt feverish, her head pounding.

Anders led the way out of the side door closest to the table, motioning to the royal blue settee in the hall.

"Do you want to go to your room and rest?" Her head of security made it very clear from his tone what he wanted her answer to be.

"I'm fine, really."

"Dani, you're shaking," Libby pointed out. "Add that to your hands glowing, clearly you're not fine."

"I don't feel the best," Dani grumbled. "Whatever's making my hands glow is making me sick."

"Sick?" Libby repeated.

"I feel like I'm burning up," Dani explained.

"Like when you're about to create sparks?"

Dani nodded.

"Perhaps Cornelius should come and do an examination?" Anders suggested.

Cornelius was the royal doctor who'd been working for Dani's family longer than she'd been alive. He'd been the one to actually assist in her and Will's births.

Dani liked Cornelius, and he made sure to keep her entertained with stories and jokes every time she had checkups—which were very frequent, thanks to her nightmares—but she despised being fussed over constantly.

"It might just be an energy surge. That's happened before."

Dani knew that she had more power than any other brytlyn in the realm, and because of her training, she was well aware of the consequences of that position. In the past, there had been times when she'd gotten a fever or chills simply due to the overuse of her power. Though it had never affected her quite like this.

Anders did not look convinced. "Still, it's better to be cautious."

"Fine." Dani drew out the word but allowed him to leave. Fighting with Anders never achieved any success. She knew that firsthand.

Libby started braiding her ponytail, an anxious habit. "Will you be okay for a minute? I'm going to have guards alert your parents."

"Do you have to tell them?" Dani pleaded. Any chance to get her parents more overprotective would yield unfortunate results.

The last incident had added to her security team, and although Dani adored Libby, her father had been talked down from adding a handful of guards to be charged with her care.

"They deserve to know that their daughter is having a magic-induced reaction," Libby said.

"But they might cancel the party!"

"I'll make sure they know that you're not in immediate danger."

"They'll tell the Magicals!" To Dani, that was even worse.

"I'll be quick, promise." And then Libby went through the doors and disappeared into the glittering masses.

"You okay, Mystery?" Amery walked through the doors a minute later. "We just looted the dessert table. I can bring out some for you if you want."

Dani had never been seasick before, but the way that her stomach was lurching must have resembled the sensation. "Actually, could you help me up? I think I'm going to head upstairs."

Amery looked surprised, but he gave her a hand up.

Dani had only been standing for a few seconds before her legs started moving rapidly, powering her forward without a second thought as to why.

Dani didn't know what was going on. Worse, she didn't know how to stop it.

All she could do was speed toward the end of the hall.

Dani could only scream as the wall loomed closer, unable to stop her feet from moving or brace herself in any way for the impact of what was ahead.

A wall that she slammed right into before crumpling, very ungracefully, to the ground.

CHAPTER FOUR

"Dani?" A hollow voice brought her back from the peaceful, cozy nook of darkness consuming her. "Nod if you can hear me."

Dani could nod, and so she did. Her head felt sore, and a wave of nausea flooded through her when she moved.

"What happened?" Her lips felt heavier than usual, but she could move them. "Where am I?" It was possible to open her eyes, but she regretted it immediately when the searing light stung her corneas.

"You ran into a wall and went unconscious," the voice replied. "And you're currently in your bedroom."

"Oh." She grunted, her head coming back into contact with the fluffy pillows propped up behind her. "Good."

"Try not to move too much. You're hurt enough," The voice chastised. This time, she recognized it.

"Hey, Cornelius."

"Don't 'Hey, Cornelius' me. You scared me and your bodyguards half to death when we arrived."

"I'm sorry," Dani apologized automatically.

Her doctor shook his head sternly. "No, don't apologize. It's not your fault that you manifested again."

Dani perked up, trying to scramble into a sitting position but aborting due to the pain. "What?"

"The reason that you ran into the wall was because of super speed."

"But I don't have super speed," Dani argued.

"Correction: You *didn't* have super speed. Now you do."

"I'm a Speed?"

"I believe so."

Dani's brain hurt even more than the dumb aches in her bones.

"Brytlyns only get one power, I thought." In her numerous hours of research, there had never been any account of a brytlyn ever having more.

"True," Cornelius agreed. "But you've never been one to stick to the status quo of what brytlyns are supposed to do."

"Are you sure that it's not a power surge?" Dani needed to ask the question, even though it was a long shot that he was mistaken. Cornelius was as good as physicians came, which was why he only worked for the royal family.

She opened her eyes again to see Cornelius nod. "Positive. I've checked. Besides, no power surge that you've had has ever led to you gaining another power."

"So, I manifested?"

"Evidently so," he agreed.

"Isn't that supposed to be impossible?" Dani had heard that word be associated with her too many times in the last few months for it not to leave a bitter taste in her mouth.

He shook his head. "'Supposed to' is the wrong phrase."

"Well, what *is* the right phrase, then?" It was hard to not be frustrated. Dani was barely able to control one power; two would be a nightmare.

"Haven't yet," Cornelius corrected. "No brytlyn has ever manifested twice—except for you, of course—so a third isn't quite as impossible as you'd think."

Dani had manifested as a baby originally and then again in her math class months before. She didn't remember the first one, obviously, but the second had been outright traumatizing. This third time had nearly been worse.

"Who else knows?" She flopped back, staring at the mural on her ceiling, counting the clouds.

"Your parents have been alerted, of course. Anders, Libby, Will, the Magicals all know, and Lord Varron witnessed it, so he knows, as well. I believe that your friends will also be alerted, as well, considering they know about your first power."

"Is the party canceled, then?"

"No. Callan was ready to cancel it, but Amandine talked him out of it after I promised that no permanent damage was done."

That was good. She didn't want everyone to worry.
"How did everyone take the news?" Dani almost didn't want to know.

"They were all shocked, as I'm sure you can imagine. Your parents took it well, much better than they did the first time. Your bodyguards were just relieved that you were all right. Will seemed to think it very cool that you and Amery shared a power. Amery was glad that he wasn't the one who hurt you."

"What do you think this means?" Dani asked quietly, her head spinning. "What happens now?"

"I'm sure that's exactly what the Magicals are figuring out as we speak," Cornelius promised.

"They could play this off as my first power, couldn't they? Barely anyone knows that I'm a Sparker anyway, so Mom and Dad could just pretend that I manifested a while ago as a Speed, since they never specified which power I manifested when it was announced last year."

"That is a sensible plan," he agreed.

"As soon as I'm able to get out of bed, I'll let them know." Which wouldn't be anytime soon if her sore body meant anything. "How long will that be, exactly?"

"By tomorrow," Cornelius said, quickly adding, "but I don't suggest that you attend school," when Dani cheered.

"Of course." She knew it was better not to fight him on that.

"And that doesn't mean that you can overexert yourself either. Yes, you have a larger magic supply than anyone else, but you also now have two different powers that take up that magic. You need to be careful how and when you use them, at least until I can determine how they'll affect you."

"I understand." In truth, Dani understood how well she wouldn't be able to keep that promise.

She was turning fourteen in less than two months. The prophecy was supposed to start coming true when she was thirteen. If she wanted to be strong enough to stop a war, then every practice was needed.

"Good. Now, do you feel up for visitors?"

Dani did her best to nod. "Sure."

Her bedroom filled up fast.

Within a minute, Dani's parents were in the room, followed by Will.

"How are you doing, darling?" Amandine asked, her and Callan moving to the side of the bed.

"Better."

Will grinned, though concern turned it into more of a grimace. "How does it feel to be the most powerful Stallard?"

"Honestly?" She offered a pained one in return, not even trying to sound better than she felt. "Not the greatest."

"How can we help?" Callan asked Cornelius.

"For the time being, make sure that she gets as much rest as possible. Then she'll need training."

"How can I do that when I have Sparker sessions for both of my training slots?" Secret training sessions that she wasn't supposed to talk about.

Will's eyes widened with an idea, but he said nothing.

"We'll work something out," her father promised.

Amandine turned to Cornelius. "When will she be able to return to Crystalium?"

"Tuesday if Dani feels up to it."

"What if Dani trains with Amery?" Will chose that moment to speak up. "I mean, she still needs her usual training once a week, but maybe instead of two days, she can train with Amery and his instructor once a week. Wouldn't that be fun, Dani?"

If Dani had the strength, she would have slapped him. Even with movement being painful, she seriously considered it.

She and Amery were oil and water most of the time. He had too much fun annoying her and knew exactly what buttons to press to get a rise out of the otherwise perfectly composed princess. They bickered more frequently than they'd ever had an actual conversation, and now that they were in their second year of sharing a school schedule, chaos seemed to ensue every day. Nevertheless, they were friends.

"What do you think, Mom?" Dani needed her to say something. Out of her entire family, Amandine was the one with the most knowledge about her situation and the one whose opinion mattered most.

"I think it could definitely be an option," she replied carefully, each word well thought out. "We still haven't officially announced your power, so announcing that you are a Speed would most likely be our best bet."

"That's what Dani suggested," Cornelius agreed.

"It's not a bad idea," her father conceded, leaning down to grab her hand. "We'll bring it up with the Magicals, but for now, you need to just focus on resting."

"I don't like feeling restless," Dani complained.

"You, of all brytlyns, can't afford to be exhausted," Cornelius reminded her.

"Noted." Dani sighed.

"I'll keep you company," Will offered.

She shook her head. "Is everyone still here?"

Callan nodded. "Yes, but the party's ending soon, so we were able to sneak off for a few minutes."

Dani glanced up at her brother. "I'll be fine here. Just tell everyone that I'm okay."

Will nodded and followed reluctantly behind their parents out of the room.

"Is being a Speed harder than being a Sparker, you think?" Dani asked, making a mental list of everything she knew about both powers.

"The only brytlyn who would know wants me to answer that question?" He was teasing, but the reminder did make the weight on her shoulders feel even heavier.

This wasn't the first time that her magic had set her apart from everyone else. Dani wished she could believe it would be the last.

But that would be a lie, and if she had discovered anything during her tenure in Breckindale, it was that she hated lying.

CHAPTER FIVE

Dani woke up feeling more energetic than she had in her entire life. Apparently, manifesting a second power made you exhausted.

"Good, you're up," Anders said when she exited her room that morning.

"What time is it?" Dani had put on the simplest tunic and leggings she could find, tied up her hair, and put on shoes.

She didn't need to look like a princess if she wasn't leaving Elthorne.

"Ten. Late for you," he observed, sounding relieved that, for once, she hadn't been up since dawn.

"Where's Libby?"

"Clearing out from the party."

"Why?"

"Because she needed something to do." Anders sighed, making it a challenge for Dani not to laugh.

"Did Mom and Dad make any progress on the plan for school?" Dani could guarantee that Anders would be the first to know if they had.

"I haven't heard anything to report yet," Anders said. "How are you feeling?"

"Better," Dani answered first, then thought of a better description. "Weird."

"Weird?"

"I feel like I have too much adrenaline."

"You'll get used to it," Anders promised.

"Oh yeah, you're a Speed too." Dani forgot that sometimes.

"What a perfect introduction to our next topic." Anders smiled—a rare occurrence in itself.

"Which is?"

"Speed training."

Dani frowned. "I thought the Magicals haven't come up with a decision yet."

"No, but your parents have. They want you to at least have a basic understanding of the power, so you'll have training here for now."

She blinked. "With who?"

"Me."

"Really?"

Anders nodded. "They wanted someone that you trust to help you through the transition."

"I trust you more than I trust anyone," Dani agreed.

"Exactly," Dani heard Libby before she saw her bounding down the hall.

"I trust you too," she promised.

Libby waved her off. "I know, but you're not an Icer. The better you learn control over this power, the more you can depend on it. There's a reason that most royal guards are Speeds."

"Because they have better reflexes?" Dani guessed.

"Speeds are faster in general," Anders corrected.

Libby smiled. "That's an advantage in battle."

"And in war."

Dani was sure that it was.

"This changes things, doesn't it?" Delacour hadn't been a Speed. Dani was supposed to be a carbon copy of her many times great aunt.

Libby nodded. "Sure, but it's a good change. This gives you a leg up."

Dani needed every advantage she could get if she was going to overturn a prophecy already set in stone. "So, how do I start?"

"By not running into a wall," Libby suggested.

"Hilarious," Dani deadpanned.

"By understanding what magical speed actually does to you," Anders corrected.

"What does it do to you?" Dani asked, following her guards toward the staircase.

"It gives you adrenaline, essentially, a very intense dose of it."

"That's good," Dani said.

"Good when it's in use, slightly difficult to manage. If you're not careful, you'll end up losing control of yourself and crashing into walls like you did yesterday."

"Oh, fun."

"All powers require some form of practice, Dani, or else training wouldn't be required at Crystalium." Libby sighed.

"I don't have the best track record with control."

Anders nodded. "Well, you're not terrified, so as far I'm concerned, you are already doing better than last time."

Libby narrowed her eyes. "I take it the last time you manifested, it didn't go well?"

"Anders didn't tell you?" Dani had assumed that Libby had been filled in on the incident months before when she'd been chosen for the job. Then again, they'd never talked about it.

Libby shook her head, her blonde braid swinging. "All I heard was it happened on earth and so you had to be moved immediately."

"I almost electrocuted my entire math class … and Grennet," Dani explained.

"You arrived only about a half hour later," Anders continued.

"I wasn't exactly thrilled about the move."

"You panicked when you found out you had a bodyguard," Anders recalled.

"Because it wasn't normal," Dani protested. "And I got over it."

"And now you aren't petrified of being a Sparker."

"I didn't have much of a choice," Dani replied bitterly. The prophecy had taken that from her, alongside a chance at a normal life in any realm with magic or without.

"But you're handling it well," Anders promised sincerely.

"Thanks." Dani had never been good at accepting compliments. "Now, how do I stop myself from running into a wall again?"

"I'm not going to have you practice while you're on the stairs."

"That's probably smart." Dani wouldn't put it past herself to trip and fall if she couldn't control what her body was doing.

Once they were safely in the foyer, Anders finally relented. "Every time that you move, you'll always have the ability to harness your speed into energy. That doesn't mean that you should."

"I don't think I've ever seen you use it," Dani remarked, glancing at Libby to confirm.

"Because there hasn't been a need to use my speed yet," Anders said. "But if there is a direct threat to you, I can and will harness it. Watch." He started as if he was going to walk to the other side of the foyer, but he shot forward in a blur instead, zipping around from corner to corner without hitting a single thing.

"I can do that?" Unlike her bodyguard, Dani had barely any coordination whatsoever. In her physical education session at Crystalium, she only got by because the skills depended more on magic than actual athletic ability.

"If you practice and commit yourself to working hard."

That she could do.

"Sir, this arrived for you," a guard reported, handing Anders a piece of parchment.

"Thank you," Anders nodded, reading the parchment before handing it to Libby.

"Well, this will be interesting." Libby snorted, grinning.

"What will be interesting?" Dani wondered, switching her gaze from one guard to the other until Anders decided to finally answer.

"You and your brother are the guests of honor for a Lirelight."

CHAPTER SIX

"What's a Lirelight?" Dani asked as soon as the unfamiliar word had processed in her brain.

"It's a tradition to celebrate a brytlyn reaching the age of fourteen and officially having a power. It's a very special party, essentially."

"And Will and I were invited to one?" Evidently, one was being held in their honor, and she really didn't know how to feel about it.

"No, you two are being thrown one at Elthorne on your birthday."

"So, it's a birthday party?" Dani wondered.

"No, it's a Lirelight."

"I'm incredibly confused."

"It'll make more sense when you're at yours. It's not really the easiest to explain until you've been to one," Anders explained.

"Why didn't Everett and Eldridge have one?" The Callisto twins had already turned fourteen.

"It's a big event with a lot of preparation and fanfare. Some brytlyns don't always want one. Fortunately, you're used to being in the spotlight, so you'll do fine."

Dani despised being the center of attention. She was sure she wouldn't enjoy this.

"And before you ask, no, you can't get out of it." Anders knew her too well.

"I wasn't even going to—"

"Liar." Libby fake coughed.

"Okay, fine. I won't try to get out of it anymore. Happy, Libby?"

"Sure. I'm just excited for your makeover."

Dani froze. "Makeover?"

"A Lirelight is a big deal, especially when it's a royal one. You'll get a brand new gown for it and hair and makeup." Libby was practically glowing with excitement. "Doesn't that sound like fun?"

"I already got a makeover when I got here. Why do I need another?" When she'd arrived in Breckindale the year before, Dani had traded her jeans and sweater for gowns in pink, purple, and blue pastels alongside pearls, jewels and a tiara.

"Because this will mark your first birthday with magic. Officially, you're still a kid, but you've been given your brytlyn birthright now. In society, you've come of age," Anders explained.

Dani wrinkled her nose. "How drastic is this makeover?"

Libby shrugged. "Not too drastic, but you'll look more made up than you do for balls and special events. Definitely more makeup than I usually put on you, and I had to wear this awful bun for mine, so tight that I couldn't move my face."

"Don't traumatize her." This time, Libby was on the other side of the infamous Anders look.

"Dani asked the question!"

"Well, I probably won't get to attend this anyway. The prophecy is supposed to come true when I'm thirteen."

"Which I brought up during the discussion about this event, but the realm has been incredibly peaceful with no issues related to rebel groups," Anders informed her.

"You knew this was coming and you didn't tell me?"

"I was waiting for the official confirmation." Anders nodded toward the parchment Libby still held.

Dani let that sink in before switching over to the other information she'd learned.

"There really hasn't been any rebel activity yet?"

Dani's smile almost lit up with hope.

Almost.

She wanted to believe it—she really did—but prophecies didn't not come true … though that was The Golden Eagle's plan. Her council believed that they could target the rebels before any chaos ensued, therefore changing the prophecy and preventing Dani's sacrifice.

It was a good plan. Dani just seriously hoped that it would work.

"None," Anders promised, already knowing exactly where her mind was going.

"The Lirelight is super important to my future?"

"Yes," Libby agreed.

"Then I won't complain too much if it actually ends up happening."

Anders looked relieved. "Good. Then we can continue your first lesson."

"You'll show me how to do what you did?"

"No, that takes more practice than a few minutes. Our goal for today is making sure that you understand the fundamentals of the power."

"What if I do amazingly well today?" Dani questioned.

"I'll think about it."

"You just want to be able to brag to Amery about this, don't you?" Libby teased.

"Of course I do," Dani retorted. Though he would probably make it a joke about how talented she was anyway and how she was making everyone look bad.

That reminded her … "Anders, you're just going to have to brag about what an incredible Speed I am when I see him next."

Anders shook his head curtly. "I am not encouraging the rivalry between you and Lord Varron."

"Why not?" Libby asked, crossing her arms. "It's entertaining."

"You were the one who encouraged me to be friends with him anyway," Dani reminded him.

"Yes, and I'm very glad that you are friends, as am I glad that you have a very good group. Even if they seem to find trouble."

"That's just the boys," Libby said. "Dani and Lydia are the ones who get them out of it."

Dani had never almost gotten herself into detention so many times in her life.

Lunch was a circus, especially at their table. And Amery always did seem to start it—not a hard task, considering he sprinted to the cafeteria every day.

"You have fun," Libby conceded.

"Yeah, I do. It's just sometimes very chaotic." As was expected by a group made up of royalty and noble kids with a penchant for pranks.

She wouldn't have it any other way.

CHAPTER SEVEN

"You look bored," Will told her that afternoon when he returned to Elthorne.

"Because I am." Dani sighed, sitting up from her current position on one of the library sofas. It didn't happen easily, especially in a palace with so much to do, but after her hour-long practice with Anders, she'd grown slightly bored of just walking around.

"Did you hear that we're having a Lirelight on our birthday?" She changed the subject to the most interesting news she'd heard all day.

Will nodded. "Yeah, Mom just told me. At least we can suffer together."

"Libby said it was a gala of some sort?"

"It's supposed to be a celebration of us having magic, but really, it's full of speeches about our journeys, and then there's this dance that we have to participate in."

"So, it's kind of like a ball?" Dani reasoned.

"Yeah, but everyone is there for us, and it's not only the nobility that goes. We get to choose the guest list ourselves."

"That's a plus side. I was told that a makeover is involved."

"For you, maybe. I don't think there's much that I need made over."

"Hey, if I'm being tortured, then I'm bringing you down with me. Anything else that I need to be aware of?"

"I think there's a demonstration of our powers, but the only one that I went to was our cousin's when I was, like, seven."

"Hopefully, I'll be ready to speed around by then. I did pretty well today."

"How much did you practice?" Will frowned. "Mom told me that Anders taught you a lot today."

"He did. And we only practiced for an hour. I just also practiced with my sparks."

"Dani!"

"I know, I know, but I just wanted to see if anything changed."

"Changed," he repeated.

"Now that I have another power, I wanted to see if it was harder or easier to use my sparks," Dani clarified.

Will took a seat on the opposite sofa. "What was the verdict?"

"It was a bit harder, but other than that, my sparks were normal. A little brighter but not necessarily stronger or faster."

"That's good, right?"

Dani shrugged. "It's confusing, but I haven't been to school, so I haven't had a chance to ask Sir Hugo about it."

"It's only been a day. I'm sure you'll figure this whole new power thing out."

Dani hoped so.

"Anyway, since I'm about to have an allergic reaction to the amount of books in here, I'm officially calling a sibling adventure!"

"A sibling adventure to where?" Dani was sure the answer was one she wasn't going to like. "Because I already went to the dungeon with you yesterday, and it's going to take a lot of bribery to get me back there."

"To Greenaway House. The Callistos headed over right after school, and I promised I'd make sure you came too."

That actually did sound fun, and seeing her friends would be nice, but … "I don't know if I'm really allowed to leave." Even to go to Amery and Lydia's house.

Will frowned. "Why not? Mom and Dad are with the Magicals right now, and you were allowed to train."

"Let me check with Anders." Libby was assisting a separate patrol for the afternoon.

"Cool. While you do that, I'll get changed and get out of this fortress of book doom." Will added a few fake coughs to further his dramatics and then walked out.

"Greenaway House?" Anders asked, walking in.

Dani nodded. His sigh seemed endless. "Do you think you can handle a blink?"

"We usually take the coach." Greenaway House was close to Umbergrove, and they took the coach to both estates.

"Your parents need it for tonight. They have an engagement."

"Oh." Dani hadn't seen her parents all day. But she was feeling better, and even if she was tired, she didn't feel drained. "Yeah, I think that I can blink."

Anders didn't seem completely convinced, but he didn't argue either. "I think it will be good for you to spend time with your friends."

Dani grinned.

"You do realize that you'll have to spend time with a group of very energetic teenagers. Your personal favorite group, I'll add."

"I can handle them," he promised.

Dani nodded. "You put up with me every day."

"It's my job," he retorted.

"And you are great at it," Dani agreed.

"And you aren't that difficult."

Dani gave him a look.

"Fine. Most times, you aren't difficult."

"Thanks."

"I assume Will rushed out to change out of his uniform?"

Dani shrugged. "Yeah, and his phobia of reading got too much."

"It's a wonder he sits still in school."

"He's good when he has to be, I guess."

"But he's allergic to books."

"He's insane," Dani retorted. "And aren't you supposed to be on my side?"

Anders shook his head. "Not with sibling debates; you're on your own for those."

"But I'm usually right!"

"Exactly. You balance each other out. That's good."

"Because he's the fun one and I'm the quiet one?"

"No. Because he helps you be a normal teenager and have fun, and you mellow him down when he needs it."

"I'm not a normal kid, though."

"You are normal, Dani. You just also have a lot more to deal with than others your age."

"I'm lying to practically everyone I know."

"To protect them."

"I still don't understand that part of it," Dani admitted.

"I know." Anders had already heard that numerous times. He never seemed to get mad at her about it, though.

"I know the order has to stay hidden and all, but if I could at least tell Will and my friends, maybe they could help. They already know more than the entire realm does about me, and they've proven that they're trustworthy."

"Your council said that they would discuss it," Anders reminded her patiently.

They'd clearly not reached a consensus then because that promise had been made only days after she had first met them.

"It's not like I really want to involve them in the dangerous parts, but they could still be helpful. Moral support, at the very least."

"You have a very talented and very loyal group around you. That's a good thing, and I, for one, am glad. I do not think that your council is keeping them in the dark to punish you."

"I would hope not," Dani grumbled.

"That is also for your protection, Dani, whether you believe you need it or not. And before you bring up that they can't protect you from the prophecy, remember that we've already had that debate."

They had. Way too many times.

"I still don't like it," she argued.

"I know, and I also know that your mother dislikes having to keep it from your father."

Dani had reminded herself of that numerous times since her first ball, especially when she was around Amandine. It had taken some time for her to get over the fact that her mother was a member of a secret society, inactive operative or not.

Sometimes, Dani felt like an outsider, even if she did know more than her brother and dad.

There were times when her mother was unavailable because she had royal business to attend to or she claimed she was ill, the latter of which was few and far between to avoid suspicion.

Dani was proud of herself for knowing when she was truthful and when she wasn't. At times it truly did feel like the only power she possessed.

The irony of the situation wasn't lost on her.

She may have been born to be the most powerful brytlyn to ever live, but it was hard not to imagine herself a caged bird.

In the grand scheme of things, Dani was the most powerless one of them all. And there was nothing that she could do to change that… except do the absolute impossible.

CHAPTER EIGHT

Dani had forgotten how much she loved Greenaway House.

Although two of her closest friends lived there, most of the time their friend group hung out at either Elthorne or Umbergrove.

Still, Greenaway House was incredibly beautiful. It was taller than it was wide, the roof of the mansion a stained glass dome in vivid blues and greens that basked the entire house in a colorful glow. Dani couldn't help finding it amusing that everyone looked like aliens when they entered the home.

Dani made it about two steps into the foyer before Lydia rushed over, engulfing her in a hug. "I can't be left alone with the boys ever again!"

Dani smiled. "Nice to see you too."

Amery dropped to one knee and bowed his head. "The queen has returned to grace us with her presence."

Everett and Eldridge snickered as Dani rolled her eyes and patted his head. "Glad to see one day without me hasn't driven you mad just yet."

Amery rose, grinning. "Close. I almost fell asleep in history this morning."

"Amery!" Lady Idalia reprimanded from the hall.

"Almost, Mom! I said almost."

"This is why he needs you," she told Dani with a weary shake of her head, heading toward the main room of the house.

"Turns out, having no one threaten me during morning announcements doesn't really help me focus in class."

Amery was one of the most popular kids in their grade and could make conversation with practically anyone. "We've only been back at school for a month. Why don't you try to make some friends?"

"Believe it or not, Amery is shy," Lydia stage whispered to Dani, who snorted in disbelief.

There were many words Dani could use to describe Amery Varron, but shy was not one of them.

"So, how are you feeling?" Amery asked.

"A lot better," Dani said. "I just have a lot of energy now."

"But you are okay, right?" Eldridge questioned. "Manifesting didn't change anything?"

Out of the corner of her eye, Dani saw Amery shrink slightly.

She shook her head. "No, I'm all good. I practiced both of my powers today and I could use them fine." It still felt weird to say.

"And the blink was all right?"

Dani nodded, glad she didn't answer when her own feet lost comprehension of gravity for a second. She would've fallen had Everett not nudged her back.

"Are you sure that you're okay?" No one looked convinced.

"Positive. I guess the blink made me a bit dizzy is all."

Dani could tell that they weren't totally convinced, so she changed the subject to something that would keep them all distracted. "Is it Turret Time?"

Lydia's eyes lit up with excitement. "On your marks!"

The first time that Dani had visited Greenaway House, it had been explained to her by the boys that since they had been little, the four of them and Lydia would always race each other to the turret, and the loser had to accept a dare that the other kids came up with.

"Get set." Everett lined up to the left of Lydia while Eldridge and Will took her right—the same order they'd had for years now. Dani walked over to stand beside Everett and prepared for the imminent stampede caused by the six of them launching themselves down a hallway to get to the staircase and then sprinting full force to the small door awaiting them beside the office.

Dani had just enough time to watch Leo and Anders exchange a wary glance before Amery cleared his throat and yelled, "Go!" giving the all-clear for the race to begin.

And begin it did.

With Amery in the lead and Eldridge and Lydia fighting to get ahead of Will and Everett, who were still way ahead of Dani, all six of them bounded down the hall, nearly taking down two paintings and an ornate vase in their wake.

Dani expected Amery to win because of his power, and if she felt confident enough in hers, she probably would have used it too. Speed would have been helpful when she was able to maneuver beside Will as they reached the turret door and its small staircase, but she fell behind once again and prepared herself for defeat.

It would be a lie to say that she handled losing gracefully, though Dani wasn't sure that anyone would when they lost to an extremely competitive group of magical teenagers.

"Okay." Dani held her hands up in surrender. "What's my dare?"

Lydia held up one finger. "Team huddle!" She pulled the boys into a circle to plot whatever doom they were going to put Dani through. Dani stood silently, just hoping the punishment wasn't as bad as Everett having to recite a historical fact every time any member of the group mentioned sparkles for the entirety of dinner.

Dani thankfully didn't have to await her sentencing long, as by the time she counted to forty, the huddle was broken. The boys and Lydia nodded at each other with smug grins.

"Well?"

"Us judges have decided that we would like to play a game," Lydia announced, her role as spokesperson having been cemented far before Dani arrived.

"Oh, good." A game with those five would either be the most chaotic experience of her life or end in a long debate over the winner. Dani had seen both.

"To honor your loss, we'd like to play Hide and Seek," Everett continued, to the applause of the four others.

Dani sighed. "I knew I'd regret teaching you guys that game."

Brytlyns had their own type of games, and Dani had learned a good number of them from her brother and friends. Dani did enjoy them, but she much preferred the human games that she'd grown up with, all of which she had explained to her friends—and all of which they had played and become obsessed with.

"But because we aren't totally heartless, we will allow one person to help you seek."

Dani chose to be positive. "Do I get to choose?"

Lydia insistently shook her head. "No, this is a part of your punishment."

"Fantastic."

"Don't be like that, Mystery. I'm a great partner!" Amery walked right over and held up his hand for a high-five.

Dani left him hanging.

"You have a minute to hide, per usual," Dani instructed her friends. "Time starts now."

They dashed away, and Dani closed her eyes. She always counted in her head, but Amery wasn't one for silence.

"I'm sorry." He said the two words that Dani would have never imagined exiting his mouth. She opened her eyes ten seconds earlier than was fair.

"For what?" she asked before announcing that time was up and that they were coming to start seeking.

"For you getting hurt." Dani could count on one hand the number of times she had seen Amery be this serious.

She followed him out of the turret and back to Greenaway House's second floor. "That wasn't your fault. It happened really fast. I don't think there was anything you could've done."

"I'm a Speed too. I could've used my power to stop you from using yours."

Dani shook her head as she led the way into the small upstairs sitting room, glancing around the sofas for any of her friends. "That would have only gotten you hurt too. I swear I'm fine."

Amery didn't look convinced. "So, you're really going to admit that you didn't freak out when you woke up and found out that you manifested again?"

All of Dani's friends had heard the story of both of her manifesting experiences at least a dozen times. They knew how terrified she'd been when sparks shot out of her hands and Grennet had whisked her to the principal's office.

"I handled it better this time," Dani told him, proud that she meant it.

He attempted a smile, but Dani could tell he wasn't going to let it go.

"It's not your fault, you know," she promised him. "Me manifesting."

Amery cracked his knuckles. "You ran into a wall, Mystery."

"Because I didn't know how to handle my own speed. That had absolutely nothing to do with you," Dani promised.

"You think it's a coincidence that a Speed helped you up and then you got the same power right after?"

"Technically, I think I manifested right before that, but even if it wasn't a coincidence, you couldn't have made me manifest or anything. That's not how it works."

"No, it's not," Amery said.

"See, looks like we actually agreed on something for once. I think this should go in the history books."

"As the first Damery agreement ever?"

"Yeah … Wait. Damery?"

Amery nodded. "Every awesome team needs an even cooler name. Though I suppose I could agree to the Amazing Incredible Brilliant Lord of Awesomeness and Princess Spark if you'd prefer."

"Absolutely not," Dani told him.

"Team Damery it is!" Amery decided assuredly, already striding ahead to the empty library. "Come on, Mystery. We have people to find."

"Coming!" she called, hurrying to catch up.

Amery seemed to have a knack for finding people, spotting Everett nestled in between two of the bookshelves in the library, then Lydia in her closet in a gigantic pile of clothes that she insisted she was going to put away, Will underneath the desk in the guest room, and finally Eldridge behind the grand piano.

Dani had only found one, which hardly counted because it was just Everett again; he had run off right after Lydia had untangled herself from the mountain of clothes she'd created. Dani couldn't tell if he had forgotten the rules or just didn't want to be crowned the loser of the game.

"This isn't how the game works," she'd lectured the second he was spotted under Amery's bed.

"I know. This is practice," he said, scooting his way to freedom.

She offered Everett a hand up and helped him to his feet.

"Good game," she told him.

"I did win, though, didn't I?"

Amery, Will, and Eldridge all argued at once about how wrong he was.

Lydia was filing her nails.

"So, does this mean I have to be a seeker now?" A trend that Dani had been very familiar with on earth was that no one ever seemed to want to be the seeker. Dani did agree that hiding was more fun.

"Yep. Tough luck," Dani told him before her smile faded and she recoiled.

Her friends were outlined in bright jewel-toned auras, surrounding each of them like color-changing shadows.

"You okay, Mystery?" Amery reached out to steady her, but Dani jerked away before he could.

"This may seem like a really dumb thing to say, but I think you guys are glowing."

"Glowing?" Lydia repeated, furiously glancing around like she herself was seeking. "We aren't glowing, Dani."

"You aren't?" Maybe the blink had affected her more than she thought.

"No." Will drew out the word, glancing first at her and then at Anders, catching his eye. "What are you seeing?"

"I don't know how to describe it. Like, colorful outlines around you. I'm not sure."

"Maybe running wasn't the best idea, Mystery," Amery said. "You may not be back to normal after your little incident with the wall yesterday."

Dani nodded, though she would have fallen had Eldridge and Lydia not grabbed her hands and steadied her.

"Yeah." The auras dissolved instantly, putting everything back to normal. "I'm fine; might just be an effect of having two powers now. It's all good they're gone now."

None of her friends looked convinced. Instead, they all backed away slowly like she was a spooked animal ready to pounce.

"What's wrong?" Dani regretted the words the second they came out, her tone sounding all wrong.

Everett turned to Eldridge. "Can light spread?"

Eldridge was even paler than usual. "No."

Dani stared down at her hand, now holding a ball-sized sphere that looked like the sun.

"Did she just …" Everett elbowed Will, who nodded.

"She just created Light," Eldridge agreed.

Dani made the rational decision to let herself freak out later. "Eldridge, how do I shut it off?" Her voice was dangerously close to frantic.

"Make a fist," Eldridge instructed.

Dani did, focusing on her breathing so that the control that she had worked hard for with Sir Hugo wouldn't come spiraling apart.

"You're good now, Mystery," Amery promised.

Anders walked over ~~calmly, placing a~~ hand on her trembling shoulder. "I think it might be best if we go home," he told her quietly.

When Will made a move to follow, Dani stopped him, rushing to block his path. "No, it's okay. You should stay and have fun."

"Positive?"

Dani nodded.

A lot happened in a minute, and Dani counted every single second.

Lydia went to grab two gemstones for blinking, Amery went to go tell his mom in case she asked why Dani was leaving, Will was talking with Anders, and Dani stayed right where they'd left her. She refused to take even another step, terrified of what could happen if she did.

She was too scared that if she moved, everything would fall apart.

CHAPTER NINE

Deja vu was never fun.

It was significantly less fun when both situations seemed to be identical in every aspect and made your head spin and hands clammy.

Dani had never wanted a repeat of the crisis meeting she'd been at the center of after the prophecy had been found, curled up on the sofa surrounded by her family while the Magicals stood in a line in front of her, offering a promise of finding a solution.

The only difference this time around was that the crisis was her now having three powers and that it was late afternoon instead of midnight.

The minute Dani and Anders got to Elthorne, everyone knew that something was wrong. Libby was summoned immediately, and Anders made Dani promise to stay in the main room until he came back. That was fine because Dani didn't feel like going anywhere anyway.

She wasn't sure how many minutes had passed before Callan and Amandine rushed in, looking perfectly regal and very, very worried.

Dani offered her best explanation, and her father had sent for the Magicals. Within ten more minutes, the entire council was facing her in their usual line.

"So, just to make sure we get this correctly, you manifested yesterday as a Speed and now today as a Lighter?" Grennet checked.

Dani nodded.

He blew out a breath. "Well, that's definitely something."

"How fast did it happen this time?" Ronan asked.

"I'm not really sure," Dani admitted, doing her best to stay calm. "First, I started hallucinating, and then everything went back to normal, but I created light."

"What things did you see when you hallucinated?" Giselle asked.

"Colorful shadows."

Iris scoffed. "Colorful shadows?"

"Or outlines, maybe … it's hard to explain. Everyone had a certain color around them."

"That sounds like the auras that Sensors use to read emotions," Cordelia decided quietly.

Dani did not like the implication.

"Were the colors bright?" Edon narrowed his eyes.

Dani nodded.

"That sounds exactly like what I see," Milos mumbled, earning nods from the rest of the high councilors.

"You think that I'm a Sensor too?" That would mean that she had manifested three new powers in two days.

"It's a definite possibility." Callan nodded his agreement.

If Amandine was surprised about this development, she didn't show it. "Could you explain more about what happened?"

And so Dani did. "We were all playing a game. I helped Everett up, and then I started feeling dizzy, so Eldridge and Lydia steadied me. Right after that, I started seeing the auras, and then they went away and the light appeared."

"Everett's a Sensor, isn't he?" her father asked. "And Eldridge is a Lighter?"

Dani nodded. Lydia was a Glamour, meaning that she could change her appearance and voice to look and sound like whoever she wanted. At the rate this was going, Dani expected to look like a Magical in the next few minutes.

"So, you made physical contact with Everett, then Eldridge, and then you manifested those specific powers in that same order?" Giselle narrowed her eyes.

"Yes." Dani's mind already flashed to her conversation with Amery. "Powers can't transfer, can they?"

"Not to our knowledge, but your magic works differently than any other brytlyn's."

Dani curled her hands into fists. "So, what you guys are saying is I'm a magnet for powers now, that I can manifest all of them at some point?"

"Well, you haven't manifested all powers yet, have you?" Iris smiled and Dani bit back a very snarky reply.

Giselle gave Iris a side eye. "She manifested three more in a span of twenty-four hours in addition to the one she's already had for thirteen years. Normal conventions are off the table."

"Yes, but only when she was with certain brytlyns. Yesterday, she was surrounded by the entire nobility, and nothing happened until she was with young Lord Varron."

Dani frowned, replaying that first conversation with Amery over and over until something clicked.

Then she found it.

"I touched his hand."

"What?" Iris said the word as if it pained her.

Dani chose to ignore the tone altogether. "I made him help me up so I could go to my room, and then right after, I got super speed."

"So it is physical contact."

"Guess so," Dani admitted, tucking her knees up so that she was farther away from her parents. "And I guess I have to be conscious for it to be absorbed because Cornelius isn't a Speed, and he did a full examination."

"So, while you are awake, any physical contact that you have with any brytlyn will trigger a new power. Evidently, the hold breaks when you have physical contact with someone else."

"And what does that mean, exactly?" From the looks of it, Amandine wasn't the only one who wanted clarification on the matter.

"It means that we don't know what it means," Grennet answered simply.

Dani did not find it comforting for the high councilors to not know what was going on.

If the Magicals were correct, then not only did she potentially have access to every power Brytlyns had ever manifested, but she could manifest every time she touched someone else or if anyone touched her.

Dani forced herself to focus on anything that wasn't panic, clamping her fists together to block the sparks just waiting to explode around the room to commemorate the moment.

Of course, that was incredibly difficult to do when Edon cleared his throat and announced, "Congratulations, Dani. You have a brand new power."

CHAPTER TEN

"A brand new power," she repeated, her voice barely a whisper.

"No brytlyn has ever been able to absorb powers through physical touch before; therefore, it's a new power." If Iris realized her annoyance was thinly veiled, she made no move to appear polite.

"I think she's just shocked," Grennet told her, offering Dani a wink.

She managed a smile back.

"Sorry. It's just a lot to take in," Dani agreed.

"What would you like to name it?" Giselle interrupted a second before Iris began.

"I get to name it?" Dani had always figured that the names of powers were picked by the ruling Magicals at that time. Other than Delacour choosing to be a Sparker, obviously.

"Well, it is yours," Callan encouraged. "When this goes in the history books, everyone should know who had the power first."

Dani hadn't actually considered that she'd make history for anything other than her destiny. The fear she was trying to keep down mixed with tiny wisps of pride at the thought. "I'm an Absorber."

It was simple, fitting, and only partially made her sound like a superhero.

"Good," Milos agreed, and then the Magicals, all seeming relieved that the matter was at least majority settled, congratulated her on both the name and the power.

Dani didn't feel quite as content. "So, now that we know I'm not a Speed, what are we going to do with training?" She couldn't train in all powers with only two training periods a week.

"We could announce you as an Absorber, say that we've kept it private because of its technicalities." Arabella glanced at Callan and Amandine, probably to gauge their approval.

The only reason that Dani's original power hadn't been announced was to protect her from unwanted attention when she'd first gotten to Breckindale. Once the prophecy had come into play, the secrecy had acted as a way to not tip off possible enemies of her title. Dani was definitely more adjusted now, but announcing a completely new power wasn't something that would go over quietly.

Giselle frowned. "Or we could just stick with our original plan of announcing Dani as a Speed. I fear that everything we've hoped to avoid through not making a public announcement about her magic will come true if we share that she is an Absorber. We've been able to keep her sparks a secret for months now, and as long as we put Dani in Speed training, then no one would be the wiser."

"It's not technically a lie," Dani said quietly. "I'm a Speed at certain points now."

That would take getting used to.

Iris let out a laugh. "Are we seriously agreeing to let her return to school? She could bump into one person and set fire to half the school."

"You're suggesting we keep her at Elthorne?" Giselle challenged, her voice raising a decibel. "She's not a weapon of mass destruction; she's a teenager."

Dani mentally thanked her.

Iris glared. "In her current state, the princess is a danger to everyone around her. She has a power that none of us marginally understand and no control over the amount of magic that it gives her."

"Well, then, I'll just have to learn to not absorb," Dani decided, silently considering the amount of trouble she'd get into for shooting sparks straight at Iris and making her flail like a spooked animal. If it didn't prove the point Iris was making, Dani would have accepted the risk.

"Powers can't be turned off once they manifest," Ronan reminded her.

"I learned how to control my emotions for my sparks. Can't I just learn not to tap into the extra powers that I get from absorbing?"

"Possibly," Edon confirmed.

Iris narrowed her eyes. "Possibly?"

"There is no way to tell since you are the only one with this power. If you were going to try, the attempt would have to be made in a controlled environment," Arabella amended.

"So that she doesn't run into another wall?" Iris was on the verge of outrage now.

"That wasn't her fault," Giselle argued.

"No, and she still injured herself. Imagine what she could do with ice or if she teleports."

"I don't want to teleport anywhere," Dani promised quickly.

Iris, unfortunately, had been prepared for that. "That may be, but if you are walking side by side with classmates in the halls of Crystalium and you accidentally bump into one, you don't really get much of a choice."

If Dani felt more like arguing, she would have brought up that she really didn't have any choices.

"I understand that there are risks at school," Dani told her finally. "But I'm around people pretty much everywhere, and keeping me at Elthorne would make me go stir crazy."

"You are not locking up my daughter," Callan ordered, putting the suggestions firmly at rest.

"Forgive me, Your Majesty. I didn't mean to insinuate the princess deserves to be locked up. I simply meant that the students of Crystalium deserve to be safe."

"And we both very much agree on that front," Amandine promised, her tone more polite than Dani had expected. "However, I believe that an alternate solution would be more beneficial for my daughter than putting her in exile for something that is not her fault."

"What should we do, then?" Cordelia beat the rest of the high council to the question.

"Give her gloves," the Queen suggested.

"Gloves?" Dani repeated, staring blankly at her mother.

"If your hands are covered, no physical contact can be made," Amandine explained.

"Gloves could work," Giselle agreed, looking relieved.

"Passing them off shouldn't be too difficult, and I probably can't create sparks with them on, so the only issue would be training," Dani conceded.

"So, we're solving two problems. Perfect." Despite her dazzling smile, Iris looked anything but pleased.

"So, theoretically, I could go to school tomorrow?" Dani pressed.

"It's a training day, but if you're careful and explain the situation to Sir Hugo, then I don't see a problem," her mother approved.

"I'll only take my gloves off during training, and Anders and Libby will be with me the whole day to help if something happens."

Dani knew that her father was skeptical, mostly because he was so overprotective. If she could convince him, then she could convince just about everyone else in the entire realm.

"Are you positive that you are feeling up to a full day of school?" Callan checked.

"I'm much better, and if I get dizzy tomorrow, I'll go to the infirmary and then blink straight here."

Her father nodded. "If it's what you want, then I see nothing wrong with this plan."

Dani grinned, thanking him.

"I suppose that settles this matter, though I'd propose that we check in with Dani tomorrow evening to see how the gloves worked and to prepare alternate plans if needed," Grennet suggested.

"Deal," Dani agreed. "And thank you."

Good luck.

Giselle didn't look at her, but Dani nodded her way anyway.

Thanks.

She'd need it.

CHAPTER ELEVEN

"How about Glove Girl?" Amery suggested, his sixth nickname in five minutes.

"Glove Girl?" Dani knew that his way of making her feel better was humor. She would have appreciated it more if she wasn't trying to focus on what the headmistress was saying.

"Well, you already shot down Commander Glove, The Glove Queen, The Great Glove Princess, The Glorious General Glove, and Your Royal Gloveness."

"What happened to just calling me Mystery?" Dani asked, fussing at her new blue silk gloves. "Or, you know, my given name."

"Fine. If you'd like me to call you Danielle, I will, but last I checked, you despised it."

She'd walked right into that one.

"Glove Girl is fine, I guess," Dani relented. "But this isn't a joke! I'm actually stuck with these."

She'd woken up to at least two dozen pairs of wrist-length gloves on her dresser, all in different colors. Libby had suggested the royal blue pair because it would match her uniform.

"Don't worry, Mystery. You pull them off."

"Thanks."

"I'm glad you're back," he promised.

"I figured." Amery had insisted upon entering the Hall of Guidance before her so that he could announce her presence to the awaiting students. He got a kick out of it and she'd tried to smack him.

"Besides, lunch just isn't the same without you lecturing us about food fights, or pranks, or trying to sneak a potion into Headmistress Athena's tea."

Dani hid her face in her hands. "Please tell me you didn't do any of those while I was gone."

"Of course not." Everett grinned from beside Amery, only pretending to pay attention to the morning announcements. "Lydia told us not to."

Dani almost smacked him too.

"You're all impossible, you know that?"

Eldridge coughed from Dani's other side.

"Fine," Dani corrected. "Will and the two of you are impossible."

"I believe the correct term you're looking for, Glove Girl, is brilliant."

"Brilliant?" If Amery was trying his hardest to be annoying, it was working.

"Or entertaining, or hilarious, or handsome."

"I think annoying works perfectly." Dani grinned when he frowned. "Kidding. You are entertaining sometimes."

"One out of three! I'll take it!" Amery cheered, pumping his fist in celebration. "So, can you still run with the gloves, or will that put you at risk?" He'd lowered his voice, glancing around at the crowded hallway as everyone filled out.

"They block physical contact, so I should be good," Dani told him, instantly regretting it when his smile turned downright gleeful.

"Fantastic, Mystery."

Since they'd met, Amery had insisted upon racing to class nearly every day. Anders and Libby traitorously thought it was hilarious and allowed it.

"You better not cheat," she warned him, wagging a gloved finger.

Amery shook his head, suppressing a smile. "I never cheat!"

"Such a liar." Dani mirrored him, shaking her head mournfully.

"Says the sore loser," Amery shot back.

"You use your speed," Dani told him. "I can't."

Amery opened his mouth and then closed it. "Mystery, that was cruel. I felt awful when you manifested, and now you're turning it into a weapon. Did you hear what she just said, Lieutenant Bower?" He turned back to Anders.

Anders gave her a pointed look. "Dani, don't tease him."

Libby was too busy trying not to crack up to take Dani's side.

Amery applauded. Slowly and triumphantly, a smirk spread on his face.

Dani frowned. "Whose side are you on?"

"It's in my best interest to stay neutral."

"So, to translate: Anders likes me better, and so does Libby." Amery grinned.

"I never said that!" Libby objected quickly.

"Yeah, you're wrong. Besides, Anders is my bodyguard, you know."

"I met him first, you know," Amery said.

Dani sighed. "Because I wasn't in Breckindale."

"I bet I'd be a fantastic charge to look after," Amery continued on as if she'd never spoken.

Dani crossed her arms. "Seriously? This conversation again?"

"Of course. You just said that I'm entertaining."

"You are, sometimes, but you're also the top troublemaker in the school."

"One day in the realm."

Dani wouldn't have been surprised if he already was.

"I don't doubt that."

"But first, I want to be known as the coolest sidekick the Savior ever had."

"I don't have a sidekick!"

Amery smirked. "So, the incredible, amazing, handsome, brilliant—"

"And so very humble," Dani interrupted.

"That too. Astounding, genius, Lord Varron, the king of pranksters, inventor of schemes, and chief annoyer of the most powerful brytlyn in the realm doesn't have a good ring to it?"

Dani pretended to consider it. "Doesn't roll off the tongue."

"Fine. We could always shorten it to Amery, Lord of All Things Awesome and Cool."

"Hard pass," Dani deadpanned.

Amery frowned. "Why?"

"Amery," Dani glowered, "be serious."

"I'm trying to cheer you up here!"

"I know." Dani stared down at her gloves. "And I appreciate it, even if your methods are completely random."

"But useful," Amery said, "and successful."

Dani shrugged. "Yeah, I guess so."

"See? I cheered you up and am getting you safely to your tower, Mystery. Doesn't that deserve an extra dessert at lunch today?"

"Fine." Dani drew out the word as Amery cheered, earning attention from the students still walking the halls. "But you can't only get fudge cakes!" During her first day at Crystalium, Amery had gotten them both plates full of sugary treats, and since then, Dani had been trying to make sure that he didn't, for his sake and for hers.

He was already crazy enough as it was.

"Of course not; there's a limit on those," Amery told her.

"Amery!" Dani chastised.

"Kidding, Glove Girl. I'm kidding. I'll get a fruit and a vegetable too."

"You're impossible." Dani sighed.

"Hey, that could be your new catchphrase."

"What do I need a catchphrase for?"

"For when you save the realm. Didn't you tell me once that all human superheroes have catchphrases?"

Dani had said that.

But … "I'm not a superhero, Amery."

"No. Technically, you're the Savior. Same difference." Amery made sure Dani was watching when he wiggled his eyebrows and nodded insistently. "You are ultra powerful and you're going to fight villains, and according to the human extraordinaire beside me, that's exactly what superheroes do all the time."

"You're not wrong."

"See, I do listen!" Amery stopped at the tower entrance, stepping aside to let Anders lead the way up.

Dani had been about to refute that statement, but he'd already run off, weaving in between the brytlyns on their way to class.

"Ready for training?" Libby asked, following behind her as they started up the first flight of stairs.

"Not really." Dani decided to be honest. She had a lot to discuss with Sir Hugo.

A lot had changed.

She just hoped it was all for the better.

CHAPTER TWELVE

"It's a surprise, though not an unwelcome one," Sir Hugo conceded after Dani had filled him in on everything that had happened in the last few days.

"Did Delacour ever get another power?"

"No, she only had one," Sir Hugo answered. "But she also was the first to have it."

And he was second and she was third.

Dani remembered her first training session after the Winter Ball. Sir Hugo had allowed it to be more of a question and answer session … mostly because Dani still was in shock over his involvement in her prophecy and didn't trust him.

He'd explained that after Delacour had saved the realm at thirteen, she had realized that Breckindale wasn't as perfect as her parents believed it to be, and she wanted to do something about it. She had already heard the prophecy and wanted to form an organization to protect both her successor and the realm, reaching out to one of the Magicals at the time to do it. Sir Hugo was one of the only Magicals who shared Delacour's viewpoint and agreed to help her, despite believing that he couldn't be much assistance because he wasn't a Sparker.

With his permission, Delacour did something risky and completely untested: transfer magic. She shot a small dose of sparks directly to his heart—where magic first stems—and he manifested later that day. According to Sir Hugo, the transfer of magic was an ancient practice that, at times, could permanently link the magic of two people in a bond called an Implexis, but that hadn't happened in over five hundred years.

Dani had then asked why no one else knew about it, and her instructor had said that his fellow Magicals had known along with the Stallard family at the time but that it had been kept from the public because the transfer could potentially have consequences. Her council knew about it, and so did her mother and evidently her father as well, but that was it.

After that, it hadn't taken long for Dani to warm back up to her mentor. After all, he had willingly accepted another power on top of his own in a dangerous experiment for the purpose of using it to guide her.

Now, they had formed a friendship filled with trust, advice … and some mild complaining on behalf of the teenage princess who had grown into her own stubbornness in the months since she'd gained the title.

"This could be an advantage," Dani told him, fussing with her gloves again. "But I also can't actually do any magic while these are on, and without them, I could gain a power that I don't know how to use."

"Are you able to use your sparks after absorbing a power?" Sir Hugo asked.

Dani nodded. "Yes, but I had to put the gloves back on and then take them off in between."

"I don't believe that two powers can be wielded at the same time, and I have never been able to prove otherwise. Though, to be fair, I am nowhere as talented as you are."

"I don't think I can use both together. Your powers don't contradict each other like mine do." Sir Hugo's original power was as a Teleporter, and although he could telepathically transport objects around, nothing was being created like light or ice.

"But if you used a power like speed, how would it be contradictory?" Sir Hugo narrowed his eyes, beginning to pace.

"Because I have an even larger amount of magic now, enough to cover every single power ever manifested. I can only absorb and use one specific power until I neutralize it with my gloves, but the amount of magic is the same."

"How is this affecting your sparks?"

"They're faster when I manipulate them to do something," Dani said. "Brighter too."

"Are they stronger?" Sir Hugo wanted to know.

"I didn't try levitation or a spark sphere or anything. Just made shapes. Did Mom not fill you in?"

"She relayed that there was a development but offered no specifics."

Amandine technically wasn't a part of Dani's council, but she did mediate between Dani and them to share information, and she came to Blitzspire as often as she could.

"How big of a risk is this?" Dani asked. "Not being able to have sparks at all times, I mean."

"It's an acceptable risk, if that's what you're worried about."

Dani shrugged.

Sir Hugo pretended not to notice. "While it is difficult for you not to consistently have access to the power you've been training with, this also offers the opportunity to use many other powers that could prove helpful."

"Only if I learn how to use them. I might be getting Speed training soon."

"And that is smart. You should have more training."

"But I can't train in all powers. That's impossible." Dani frowned.

"No, not in all powers, but in some. Speed training, perhaps transference?"

"The only times that I can use them are after physical contact with brytlyns who wield that power. Speed is fine because Anders barely leaves my side, but the Transferer I'm usually with is my brother."

"I imagine you will be around others as time goes on," Sir Hugo promised.

"Or you and the council can finally consider my offer and let Will and my friends get filled in," Dani suggested.

"We have discussed it."

"And you've all decided against it?" Dani guessed.

"We are simply weighing our options," he corrected.

"But they already know that I'm a Sparker, and that I'm an Absorber, and all about Delacour and the prophecy."

"As do your guards, and they aren't a part of the order."

"Well, not officially."

"While I'm not saying it's a bad idea, I do think that you don't fully understand the risks of having teenagers as members of our order."

"I'm a teenager and you let me join."

Sir Hugo swiped a hand over his face. "You're also the reason that the organization was created in the first place. You're a special case."

"But they are really, really talented. Not just in magic but in history and puzzles and codes—have I mentioned that they solved yours?"

"Only a few dozen times."

"Because they did!" Dani emphasized.

"I agree. Considering everything you've told us about them and what I've heard from Amandine, you've chosen a very good group of friends."

"Who could be a great help!"

"Have you considered the hardships?" Sir Hugo questioned. "The fact that your friends will also be sworn to secrecy and unable to tell anyone else where they blink to at night or what they are doing?"

Evidently, not as much as she should have.

"Or made sure that they wanted to join?"

"Well, I can't exactly ask them if they want to be a part of a secret organization that I'm half in charge of, now can I?" Dani argued.

"No, but gauging their willingness is an important step. You were given a similar choice not long ago, and I believe that your brother and friends deserve that same opportunity, don't you think?"

"Yes." She expected that they would think of it as an adventure. A secret mission. Saving the realm and being heroes would be a welcome bonus.

"Delacour was like that," Sir Hugo said, "jumping into ideas before she fully considered the risks and consequences."

"I'm not Delacour."

"No, and you need to use that as an advantage. Now, Spark Sphere around me. Go!"

CHAPTER THIRTEEN

Dani spent half of her lunch period answering the new questions her friends had about her new power and the other half trying to not stain her gloves.

"So, how many powers do you actually have?" Everett wanted to know.

"Technically two," she answered. "But I can absorb any power as long as I have physical contact with its owner."

"And the gloves protect you from that, right?" Lydia asked.

Dani nodded. "So far."

"And you can still use your sparks?" Eldridge checked.

"Yes, but I can't use two powers at the same time. At least, I haven't been able to yet."

Lydia's eyebrows shot up to her hairline. "Could that be possible?"

"I'm not totally sure about that either," Dani admitted.

"What are the Magicals going to do?" Amery chimed in. "You made history, Glove Girl."

"Glove Girl?" Lydia rolled her eyes across the table at her brother.

"It's my newest brilliant nickname, and before you start throwing things, it's Dani approved."

"You approved it?" Lydia switched her gaze from her twin to her best friend.

"It was the best out of the other five," Dani explained.

"I'm wearing her down with my charm. I know it." Amery grinned triumphantly.

"I think she's just finally realized that fighting against one of your ideas is useless," Will interjected.

"We learned that lesson a while ago," Everett agreed.

"Uh, please. My ideas are brilliant."

"They usually end up with us almost getting detention," Lydia reminded him.
"But they never actually do because we plan so well. Really, the four of us are geniuses."

Lydia narrowed her eyes. "And Dani and I aren't?"

"At pranks you aren't."

"You always try to stop us," Will remarked.

"It's called being responsible," Lydia said primly.

"It's called being boring." Amery laid his head on Dani's shoulder, snoring animatedly before she pushed him off.

"I don't think any of us are boring," Dani argued.

With a friend group comprised of a Savior, the heir to the throne, and two sets of noble twins, it was hard to be.

Amery sighed. "Fine. I admit it, I was wrong."

"Well, that's a first." Eldridge snorted.

Will held up a fork in mock salute. "We should all take a minute to savor this moment."

"Oh, I am *never* going to forget this." Lydia's grin was an exact match for the one her twin wore like armor.

Everett shook his head. "I don't think any of us will."

Amery's cheeks went beet red.

"Score one for Team Dani!" Will fake coughed.

That seemed to bring Amery out of his embarrassment enough to feign shock. "As my best friend, you should really be supporting me!"

"I know, but she clearly takes this one, and she's my twin sister and knows where I sleep."

"I know where you sleep," Amery said, sinking a fork into his fudge cake for added emphasis. "Do our secret passageway expeditions ages eight through ten mean nothing to you?"

Everyone laughed at that, four voices erupting into boisterous chatter about childhood memories and adventures long since ended.

Dani always felt a familiar pang of loneliness when her friends or brother talked about their childhoods. She wasn't quite the outsider anymore, but more often than not, Dani couldn't relate to the stories or inside jokes the rest of her group had shared long before her arrival.

Her childhood had been good too, a thought that she had forced through her mind every time one of these conversations happened. Her human parents had been two of the most supportive and loving people Dani had ever met—brytlyns included. And she'd loved them very much. She still did love them very much.

It did make the pit in her stomach grow thinking of the number of times that Dani had allowed herself to think of them since she'd left earth. It had only been a handful.

That was one of the hardest parts of being in Breckindale: the life already ready for her.

She'd traded parents for a family and added a castle, bodyguards, actual friends, and loads of crazy magical stuff she didn't understand into the mix.

Dani would be lying if she said that Breckindale always felt like home.

She'd be lying if she said that she didn't miss earth.

She'd been normal there.
Dani wasn't sure if being extraordinary here was really any better.

You belong in Breckindale.

Dani hadn't realized Will had used his power until the message came through like a hollow echo.

I know.

But did she? Since arriving in the realm, all Dani had done was make waves and ruin the careful balance keeping brytlyns safe for a hundred years. Regardless of her destiny, both of the powers she possessed were harmful and dangerous. She was harmful and dangerous.

And the chosen one. Don't forget that.

Forgetting that was impossible, and she would have told her brother that had Lydia not laughed so hard she snorted and made the boys quickly follow suit.

Dani put a smile on her face, watching as Eldridge tried his best to continue whatever story Lydia had found so amusing.

On the outside, she looked perfectly at ease. On the inside, the voice inside her head viciously chipped away at the thin layers of confidence and belonging Dani clung to every minute of every day, listing every reason the realm was better off without her.

Despite her best efforts, the rest of lunch passed her by in a continuous cycle of forced laughter and blank faces, and if any of her friends noticed, they didn't press the issue. Dani wondered if Will had transferred messages to them too.

Anders and Libby said nothing as they escorted her to physical education, though that wasn't necessarily uncommon. Lydia took that time to fill Dani in on gossip and news she didn't want the boys to know.

Dani survived the session well enough, mostly because she was usually pretty quiet in that class anyway. The skill was vanishing—which Dani held a record for—and that didn't require much talking anyway.

That didn't stop Will from glancing over at her every time she reamerged and silently asking what she was wrong.

It was hard to explain when a large part of that explanation included a secret society that he wasn't allowed to know existed.

Dani made herself vanish for thirty-minute increments just because she could. She didn't have the energy to analyze every aspect of her life a million times over until the end of school.

"Okay, what's wrong?" Will walked beside her as they arrived back to Elthorne at the end of the school day. "You were comatose for half of lunch and then didn't speak at all on the way to the blinker."

"Nothing's wrong," Dani answered, probably too quickly.

"You do realize that every time you say nothing's wrong, it's almost always a lie, right?

Dani glared. "Thank you, Will."

"I can't help if you deflect the question."

"You can't help regardless."

Dani regretted her sharp tone when Will's expression grew clouded.

"I think moving to Breckindale was a bad idea," she finally admitted.

Will frowned. "Well, that's stupid. You've always belonged here."

"But since I've returned, everything has gotten worse. The Magicals are preparing for a war, Mom and Dad have to lie to the entire realm, and my magic is one handshake away from destroying the school."

"All of those reasons are ridiculous now and were ridiculous earlier," Will objected.

Dani crossed her arms. "Mom said that you're not supposed to read my mind."

"Well, you were in zombie mode. I figured I had to do something."

"I was thinking of my old life," Dani confessed, unsure why it felt so embarrassing to say. It wasn't a secret that she'd had a life on earth before she'd returned to Breckindale; both of them knew that. Her guards knew that. Her friends knew that.

"You miss it?"

"A little bit, yeah." Dani had never been sure if her brother would want to hear about the life that he hadn't been a part of, so they'd never talked in depth about her childhood.

"I'm sorry." Will offered what support he could. "And I'm here if you need someone to talk to about anything. That's my job as your older brother."

"You're only four minutes older," Dani reminded him, rolling her eyes.

Will shrugged. "Still counts."

"Fine, but I'm definitely more mature." Dani pretended to consider his answer.

"Considering you like to blackmail our friends into getting you extra desserts, that's definitely debatable," Will told her, leading the way up to the landing. "But because this is the most you've spoken in a few hours, I'll let it slide."

"What a considerate brother." Dani put a hand on her heart.

"I try," Will agreed.

"And you're good at it," Dani promised him. "Thank you for cheering me up."

"Anytime, and I mean that."

Dani hugged him, partially because she needed a hug herself and partially because her brother deserved one. She did, however, refuse his offer to go explore some secret passageways.

"Is it bad that I miss earth?" Dani flopped onto her bed as soon as she made it to her room.

"Of course not," Libby promised. "You lived there for thirteen years of your life; it's normal."

"But I feel like I shouldn't," Dani mumbled, tossing a pillow up and catching it.

"Because it wasn't real?" Anders guessed, setting her bag down beside her desk.

Dani threw her pillow up again. "I wasn't really human, I wasn't really their daughter, none of it was real."

"But it was real to you," Libby added gently.

"Yeah," Dani agreed, sitting back up. "It was."

She would have said more if a guard hadn't knocked on her door. "I apologize for interrupting, but Her Majesty wants to see the princess in the sitting room, and the king has requested a meeting to discuss the security plan for the Lirelight."

"She'll be right there," Libby told the guard with a nod.

"As will we," Anders added.

The guard nodded and left.

"Do you think the Magicals are already here?" Dani hopped off of her bed, confused. She had only just gotten back from Crystalium; surely, the high councilors hadn't meant to come so early.

"Only one way to find out." Libby shrugged, walking with her out to the hall. "But you didn't have any incidents at school today, so I'm betting that it won't be a bad meeting."

"Unless Iris decides to argue for an hour against me." Dani could definitely see that happening.

Libby flipped her pink-streaked hair off of her shoulder. "If the gloves worked, then she doesn't have a case."

"I really hope so," Dani muttered, heading down the stairs as her guards split off, already en route to her father's office.

She just couldn't convince her heart to stop speeding up as she approached the sitting room, nerves morphing into concern when the only person in the room was her mother.

The nerves returned the second Dani saw a flash of gold in her hand.

"Hugo needs you to blink to Frovland." Amandine handed her the medallion that was supposed to be hidden under Dani's mattress.

She smiled when Dani's eyes widened in confusion. "I grabbed it before you arrived home."

"Are you not coming?" When they blinked together, Amandine's medallion was usually the one they used, not Dani's. The Queen always kept hers on her in pockets sewn into dresses or cloaks so it was more convenient during quick visits.

"I need to stay here in case the Magicals do arrive. There has been a new development, and your council needs you there immediately."

Dani's heart practically beat out of her chest.

"Everything's fine." Her mom didn't need to read minds to know the thoughts already taking control of Dani's vivid imagination. "But you should go."

Dani nodded and, with a gloved hand, pressed down on the frost crystal embedded in her medallion and dissolved in a flash of light.

CHAPTER FOURTEEN

Dani's first thought upon landing in Frovland was that Anders was most definitely going to ground her when she got back.

She hadn't given a second thought to blinking without him and Libby, but being surrounded by the familiar blue forest made her realize that she'd promised to never go alone.

"I'm here!" Dani called out to the empty forest, far less frozen than the first time that she'd been there but just as windy.

She didn't even flinch when the whirlpool formed in front of her, a silver pool swirling round and round. Dani walked to the edge and jumped in, grateful for the months of practice when she landed in a perfect crouch.

The silver holding room still looked as sleek as it always did, though far more empty than usual.

Fortunately, she didn't have to wait long, as the tunnel opened after only a few seconds, revealing the rest of the secret base and a golden suit of armor.

"You got here fast," Radian told her by way of greeting, leading the way down the stark silver hall.

Dani nodded, hurrying to walk beside him. "Mom said it was an emergency and I got worried."

"How are the gloves working?" he asked, laughing at Dani's shocked expression. "Did you really think that Amandine wouldn't have informed us about you manifesting as an Absorber?"

"Not really," Dani decided, considering the question. "And the gloves are working so far."

Armor clanked as Radian nodded. "Where are your guards?"

"At Elthorne," Dani answered.

"Did you ditch them, or did they decide that you could come alone?"

"I forgot them," she insisted, though technically, ditching was accurate.

Radian shook his head, golden helmet barely moving. "Not going to lie, you're sounding more and more like Delacour by the day."

Dani knew Delacour had been an inspiring hero and leader during her lifetime, leaving behind a legacy dedicated to peace and prosperity, but sometimes, the comparison made her feel prickly with pressure.

She was Delacour's heir. Her hope for the future. The entire reason that The Golden Eagle existed. They may have shared a power, a title, and a prophecy, but Dani was nowhere near as fearless.

"I guess so," Dani replied, though her smile was uneasy at best.

Thankfully, she was saved from any more comparisons as they had reached the conference room, the same room where Dani had first met her council months earlier. It was also the same room where she had learned that her mother had been pulling the strings for years behind the scenes to get the prophecy to her.

The horseshoe-shaped table was nearly full when they entered. Nova, Tobin, and Scala stood behind it, their gold ensembles masking each of their identities. The only brytlyn that didn't wear a disguise was Sir Hugo.

"So, what's the new development?" Dani asked, taking her usual place beside Sir Hugo at one of the curved ends of the table while Radian went over to the other.

"Some of our operatives have noticed unusual activity near one of our most secluded hideouts," Nova answered, her golden gown shimmering.

"What kind of unusual activity?" Dani asked.

Her council turned to each other, silently debating before Sir Hugo nodded and turned back to her.

"Rebels."

Dani had known that the prophecy would begin eventually. She'd been preparing daily to grow her control, her strength, to plan in war strategy and risk assessment all for the moment when she'd need to take back her kingdom.

Fear crept in, freezing her heart and clenching it in an iron hold.

"My rebels?" She swallowed it down, forcing her voice not to shake and the hard-earned control of her sparks not to shatter.

"We believe so, yes," Scala agreed, her gold tutu looking both out of place and perfectly normal for a war discussion. "Though this only occurred this morning, so we aren't certain on all the details."

Dani had never wished to have Anders and Libby by her side more, though they wouldn't have been allowed into the room anyway.

"Why didn't you tell me about this during training?"

If Sir Hugo was fazed by the question, he didn't show it. "Because I didn't want you to panic."

Now, Dani was scarily close to panicking. She didn't feel any better.

"Are they the same as Delacour's?"

Sir Hugo shook his head. "Not quite. We haven't found a connection between the two groups, though it can't be ruled out, of course."

Dani had always assumed that since she was related to Delacour, her rebels would be too. Like a generational rivalry.

"How much do you know?"

Sir Hugo sighed. "Not as much as we'd like to, I'll admit. They appear to call themselves the Midnight Dragon, wear blue cloaks with a white flame on the back, and so far, we've seen six of them blinking to an area close to one of our Breckindale bases."

"Lovely," Dani muttered, her brain cataloging the new information before she gave herself a chance to react. "Wait, we have a base in Breckindale?"

"Yes," Tobin answered, his golden soldier uniform spotless. "Though it's used mostly for storing records and isn't used often."

Dani may have been half in charge of The Golden Eagle, but she'd never actually visited any of the other bases, despite knowing that they existed. Blitzspire was where all of the meetings that she attended were held, so there had never been a reason for her to venture to the others.

"What should I do?" Delacour hadn't saved the realm until after

The Order of the Raven had taken over and forced the royal family into hiding. Dani had never excelled at waiting.

"Nothing for now."

Dani frowned. "Nothing?"

"It is very possible that if we know about the Midnight Dragon, then the Midnight Dragon knows about you and this organization. As much as I'm sure you'd like to go and find them right this second, on the off chance that they don't know about you yet, we shouldn't go and provoke them."

"So, we're just going to let them destroy the realm?"

"Of course not," Nova promised. " We just simply want to ensure your safety if we can."

"Is my safety presently being threatened?"

Sir Hugo chose not to answer. "The Midnight Dragon will be after you the second that they know about the threat you pose to them. They will see you as the singular threat to their realm domination and stop at nothing to kidnap, harm you, or worse."

"They'll kill me," Dani filled in.

"Yes, and have no mercy in doing so. The first part of prophecy is in your favor, and that ultimately makes you a target. Delacour wasn't at that point."

"Delacour was underestimated," Dani mumbled.

Sir Hugo nodded. "No one knew about her power until after she used it. That's the reason that yours has been kept secret."

"I'm not going into hiding with my family or watching my friends turn against each other."

"We understand that," Scala promised.

"So, you'll let me tell them?" Dani checked, crossing her fingers and hoping that they had finally made a decision.

Sir Hugo's sigh sounded tired.

"You said I made a good point earlier!" she reminded him. "And I won't let it go until you guys give it a fair shot."

"And we have," Radian interjected.

"But?" Dani was sure there was one coming.

"Our organization has never utilized teenagers, and there are certain risks that come with that."

"The organization was founded by a teenager and is currently being led by one." Dani played the one card that she felt confident in.

"And both you and Delacour were both already key to this fight before the organization entered the picture. You accepted the danger and the responsibility that came with it long before." Radian brought up a good point.

Dani was fairly certain she knew where the conversation was heading. "My friends already know that a secret organization exists. I told them after the ball that you'd just given me advice, but eventually, they'll probably figure out the truth. I guarantee all of them will want to help, and I think it is smart to let them."

"You have a very talented group of friends; none of us will discredit that," Sir Hugo began. "We have all agreed that having your friends join this order would be a fantastic help and would definitely be an asset to you. We simply are unsure of the toll that it would take on them."

"I've handled it okay, and I'm actually in charge," Dani reminded them.

"Yes, you've done tremendously well, but it took you time to adjust as well. And you've spoken about the hardships that keeping this secret has had on you."

"Because it's not easy lying to everyone all the time and having no one to talk to about it."

"Your mother shared many of those sentiments as well."

Dani had originally blamed her mother for her involvement with The Golden Eagle because she'd been keeping it from their family and working behind the scenes to ensure her daughter's fate had a fighting chance. Dani wasn't sure if it was a good thing that she'd grown to understand how much the choice had affected her.

"What if I ask them first?" she suggested quietly. "They've kept my power a secret for months. Even if they don't want to join, at least we can be certain they can be trusted."

The council said nothing else, seemingly considering the issue in silence as their Savior frowned, switching her gaze every few seconds from one advisor to another, trying to crack their expressions for a clue. It wasn't going as well as Dani had hoped.

"Fine," Sir Hugo agreed after an agonizing thirty seconds of silence.

Dani grinned.

"But you need to stay vigilant until we know more about the rebels.

We don't know who or what is leading them."

"My friends aren't traitors." That was something Dani was sure of.

"No, I don't believe they are." Sir Hugo confirmed. "But others may be."

CHAPTER FIFTEEN

"Looks like the guest of honor is finally joining us," Grennet said, his lips twitching with amusement as Dani raced into the sitting room, her medallion hastily shoved into her pocket.

"I'm sorry for being late." After some words of wisdom from Sir Hugo, Dani had blinked back to Elthorne and hurried to the sitting room as soon as she'd heard voices.

"We haven't been here long," Giselle promised. "And you clearly needed that nap."

Dani was sure that her dark circles had only increased because of her visit, but she nodded anyway, agreeing to the excuse that Amandine had whispered to her upon her arrival.

Iris puffed out an impatient breath. "Well, now that Dani has finally graced us with her presence, can we begin the meeting?"

"Of course," Dani agreed, sitting down on the sofa. Neither of her parents were in the sitting room, which meant that she had to face their council alone.

What a joy.

"I take it that the gloves were successful?" Ronan asked, glancing down at the blue silk covering Dani's hands.

"I didn't manifest at all," Dani told him, holding her gloves up to inspect them. She'd bumped into enough brytlyns in the halls to be confident in her new accessories.

Iris moved to speak, but Giselle was faster. "She's not bluffing, if that's a concern for anyone. I've read her mind and the gloves worked perfectly."

"Well, then, I don't think there is much of a debate," Milos decided.

Dani grinned. "I can still go to school?"

"I see no reason that you can't," Grennet admitted.

"Neither do I," Giselle agreed.

Dani had never been more grateful that they were her favorite Magicals.

In the end, even Iris had to agree that Dani could attend Crystalium as long as she wore her gloves every day and stayed cautious.

"Tomorrow is Wednesday," Dani realized just as the Magicals were preparing to go speak with her parents, "so I'll have regular classes."

"I don't see an issue that would require you to take off your gloves. On Thursday, you can remove your gloves for training only, just as you did today."

Dani had assumed that would have to happen.

"So, nothing is changing with training? We're just going to keep my actual powers a secret?"

"That's actually up to you," Arabella corrected. "If you think it would be beneficial to continue having both training sessions devoted to your sparks, then nothing will change."

"If not?"

"We have seriously considered simply announcing that you are a Speed tonight and having you train with that power once a week to gain mastery."

"I'm okay with that," Dani conceded. Like Libby had said, there was a good reason that the vast majority of palace guards were Speeds, and it would be helpful to know how to use a power so beneficial in battle. Especially if her enemy didn't know she had it. "But my instructor would need to know about my power if I want to use it."

"Which is why we already had a very trustworthy one picked out," her father explained, walking in with her mother. Dani wondered how long they'd been eavesdropping.

"Who?" Dani didn't know of any Speed instructors that her parents knew well enough to trust with a secret so large.

"Colette Lexington." Her mother smiled knowingly.

The name did sound familiar, but Dani couldn't place where she'd heard it until a distant memory from the previous year floated to the forefront of her brain.

Her expression turned sour when she realized just who she'd heard it from. "You want me to learn from Amery's instructor?"

Her father nodded. "And we have a way to ensure you don't have to tell your instructor about your absorbing if you don't feel comfortable doing so."

It took Dani a few seconds to realize what he meant. "You want me to have sessions with Amery?"

"You'll start Thursday." Amandine sounded far too happy about this arrangement.

"I thought nothing had been made official yet?" The Magicals had only just discussed the idea with her a few minutes before.

"Your father and I prepared the arrangements this morning so that all we needed was your approval."

"So, you actually listened to Will's idea?" Dani blinked. "He only suggested it because he wants to be a pain."

"But it's not a bad suggestion," Grennet remarked. "You can keep your absorbing a secret and still gain training with one of your powers alongside someone you already trust."

Dani couldn't argue with the logic no matter how much she wanted to.

"Fine," she begrudgingly agreed. "I'll try it."

Well, this is sure to be an interesting learning experience.

Giselle gave a hint of a smile when she transferred the message straight into Dani's brain.

The princess snorted. If only Giselle knew how right she was.

CHAPTER SIXTEEN

"I'm sorry," Dani said for what had to be the millionth time.

The Magicals had gone with her parents to draft the official announcement, and Dani had found her bodyguards waiting for her when she made it to the foyer.

"I know," was the only reply that Anders had given her during the time it had taken them to get to her bedroom.

Libby had tried to be stern, lasting an impressive three minutes before she broke, warning Dani not to do it again before standing back to let Anders begin his lecture.

And begin it he did. Anders spent so long talking that the sky was painted in vivid hues of pink, purple, and orange when he finally stopped.

Dani spent the entirety of his speech dutifully sat on her bed, waiting for a good moment to tell her guards what she'd found out.

When the moment came, she first decided to explain herself.

"I had to make a split second decision, and I didn't want anyone to see me blink."

"Which was smart of you," Anders offered words that Dani definitely hadn't expected out of his mouth. "But you've been here long enough to know that you aren't supposed to go anywhere without at least one of us with you."

"I know … and I'm sorry."

She also knew that Anders and Libby were two of a very select number of people who knew the truth of her situation. Her mother had allowed them to know about The Golden Eagle because she'd wanted Dani to have people to help and support her.

"You've mentioned that." Anders wasn't really the smiling type, but he wasn't heartless, especially not with her.

"Well, I figured you'd be mad at me."

"I'm not mad," Anders told her carefully, three more words Dani hadn't expected.

She frowned. "Why not? I snuck off to a completely different realm without telling you where I was."

"Which I should have figured you'd do eventually. You're certainly more adventurous than you were when we met. Nevertheless, I'm proud that you did it safely and made a smart, calculated decision in a hard situation. I'm simply disappointed that you didn't wait."

Anders wasn't even her father, and yet disappointing him made her feel twenty times worse. Maybe it was because she valued his opinion so much. Maybe it was because she'd already disappointed Callan once.

"Mom said that it was urgent." Dani twisted her glove.

"And was it?"

Dani ripped off the bandage, spitting out the words as quickly as she could. "Some operatives saw the rebels that might be from the prophecy around their base in Breckindale. My council thinks they were looking for me."

Libby fingers crusted with ice and she paced the length of the room twice, sheathing and unsheathing her sword. "What else do they know?"

"The rebels belong to a group called the Midnight Dragon. We aren't sure if they are connected to Delacour's enemies yet, but there's a good chance that they could be."

Libby said some very unkind words under her breath.

Anders could've withered flowers with his glare, but when he spoke, concern broke through. "How are you holding up?"

"I'm fine," she assured him, honestly not surprised that his first priority was checking on her.

"What are The Golden Eagle doing to prevent them from beginning the prophecy?" Libby questioned, as eager to end this whole thing as Dani was.

"Nothing for now. Since they aren't sure that the Midnight Dragons know about me, they don't want to put me on the radar."

"That's smart," Libby conceded, though her hand stayed by her sword. Dani swore the hilt was lightly frosted.

Anders cleared his throat. "For the foreseeable future, you will go nowhere without at least one of us beside you. That means school, home, Frovland, Umbergrove, Greenaway House, anywhere."

Dani nodded. "I understand."

"Good," Anders said, "because I'm certain that the Lirelight may be moved up because of this. That means you'll begin preparing sooner than later, and more brytlyns will be here."

"How tough is this going to be?" Dani asked.

"Tough may not be the right word," Libby corrected gently.

Anders nodded his agreement. "You'll have rehearsals, sessions with gown designers, hair stylists, run-throughs."

"I meant getting ready for war and having brytlyns out to capture and kill me, but the Lirelight stuff sounds tough too."

"It is, but you'll pull through," Libby promised.

"Will I, Libby? Will I really?" Dani flopped back on her bed for emphasis.

"Considering all style decisions are going to have to go through me, you have nothing to worry about," Libby promised.

"I'm not worried about that stuff; I just don't want them," Dani complained.

"No kidding."

Dani could practically hear Libby rolling her eyes.

"You don't have to like any of this, but you have to do it," Anders reminded her.

"So, you can't simply say that I don't want one?" The Callistos had done that, hadn't they?

Anders shook his head. "No. Would you like to guess why?"

"Because the universe wants me to suffer." Dani stared up at her ceiling mural like it held every answer she'd ever need.

"Try again." Anders did not sound as amused as Dani was with her response.

"Because the Magicals want me to suffer."

"Danielle Hope Stallard."

"Because I'm Princess of the realm and have a duty and responsibility to Breckindale that apparently involves a fancy party in my honor?"

"Third time's the charm!" Libby cheered.

Dani forced herself back into a sitting position. "And are you sure that there is absolutely no way that I can get sick and or injured before this?"

"Cornelius will fix you," Libby said.

"Oh," Dani grumbled. "Fantastic."

"You promised you wouldn't complain." Anders fixed her with a stern look, daring her to object.

Dani knew better than to argue.

"I'm not complaining. I'm just processing information that I don't like loudly."

Anders grumbled something that sounded a lot like "teenagers" and then sighed. "Do the Magicals know about the development?"

Dani frowned. "I don't think so. I didn't tell them, if that's what you're wondering about. I wasn't sure how to explain it to them without saying anything I'm not allowed to."

She didn't know if her mother knew that either. Dani wouldn't have been surprised if she did.

"They'll need to know to begin preparing," Anders told her.

Dani figured that they would. "But my council did say that I can tell my friends and Will." That, at least, was good news and all too relieving.

"How long did you argue with them this time?" Libby snickered.

"Only a few minutes. I had some pretty convincing points." Dani beamed. "Like the fact that they solved The Golden Eagle's riddle and have kept my power a secret from everyone."

"Both very valid arguments," Libby agreed.

Dani grinned. "My thoughts exactly."

"Your council is allowing your friends to join the order?" Anders questioned.

"See, join is more of a relative term here. It's up to them if they want to swear an oath and join, but they can't make that decision until after I've given them all of the facts."

"Are you going to tell Will about your mother?"

"He deserves to know." She gave herself a mental note to make sure she remembered to tell him about Amandine privately. He deserved that much.

It had hit her hard, and she'd only known their mother for a couple days. Will had years over her.

Libby nodded. "Let's be honest: There's no way that they won't join. A secret hideout seems right up the boys' alley, and Lydia likes the codes and riddles aspect of it."

"I'm guessing the Magicals said that you can go to school tomorrow?" Anders asked.

"Yeah." Dani couldn't believe she'd forgotten to fill them in on that. "And I have an update about my new power too."

"Are they announcing that you made brytlyn history?" Libby wondered, her eyebrows so high they almost got lost in her hair.

"They're announcing that I manifested as a Speed," Dani corrected.

"It will keep suspicion away from you and isn't technically a lie," Anders conceded.

"Yeah, and I'm starting my official Speed training tomorrow." She explained the new arrangement to her guards, both of whom had varying reactions to the news.

"Well, this will be fun." Libby grinned, far too excited for Dani's liking.

Dani frowned. "Bickering with Amery for an extra few hours every week?"

"No, getting to watch the two of you train together. The instructor will have a headache in, like, five minutes."

"So will I," Anders agreed, allowing himself a smile when Dani glared.

Libby curled a strand of pink hair around her finger. "I'll bring snacks."

CHAPTER SEVENTEEN

Libby hadn't been kidding about the snacks.

When Dani emerged from her bedroom on Thursday morning, Libby was the only one of her guards waiting in the hall, her hair down with tiny braids woven through the blonde and pink tresses.

"Morning," she greeted, holding a pink satchel stuffed to the brim.

Dani looked around. "Is Anders downstairs already?"

"Slight change of plans. Anders has to stay at Elthorne, so it's just me going to school with you today. I know, awesome news."

"That is awesome news," Dani agreed, starting down the hall. "But is he actually needed or just trying to get out of attending my training?"

"Officially, he's working on some security related matter for your parents, but I don't think he's devastated to miss your first speed training session today either."

"His loss," Dani lamented, shaking her head.

"Agreed. I personally can't wait to see you and Amery bicker for hours. It'll be like those human shows that you used to watch—what were they called again?"

Dani had told Libby about a lot of human shows and movies that she used to watch. There was only one type of show that Libby had found completely hilarious enough to bring up now.

"Reality shows?"

Libby's entire face lit up. "That's the one!"

"My life is not a reality show," Dani retorted.

"I'm not saying that your life is a reality show; I'm saying that training will be. Why do you think I'm looking forward to it?"

"Because you think that my feud with Amery is entertaining," Dani pretended to guess, starting down the grand staircase.

"It's not a feud; it's a rivalry," Libby corrected. "And no, I'm looking forward to your speed training because It'll be good to see you not beat yourself up over not being perfect at a power for once."

Dani arched a brow. "How do you know that I won't do that with this one?"

"Because it's impossible for you to be perfect at every single power. By training in one of them, you're taking control, and control is super important for powers, especially both of yours. Point is, you are achieving the impossible."

"Nice pep talk," Dani approved. "You're starting to sound like Anders."

"Thank you. I've been practicing."

Dani rolled her eyes.
"But that's definitely not the only reason you're looking forward to my training."

"It's not my fault that Amery is hilarious—and if you ever admit that I said that out loud, I will freeze your feet and ditch you."

Dani put a gloved hand to her heart in mock offense. "I don't think you are supposed to threaten your charge, Libby."

"I'm not threatening. I'm issuing a warning."

"Sure." Dani had been threatened by Libby a dozen times since they'd met, usually by way of frozen punishments. She was still shocked that Libby hadn't tried to freeze her the day before.

"You two may have an interesting friendship, but Amery's teasing is very effective."

"If by effective, you mean annoying, then yes, it is," Dani agreed.

Libby gave her a look. "No, Amery gets you out of your shell. He makes you laugh when no one else can. It's why Team Damery is an awesome duo."

"If you ever repeat those words, I'll shoot sparks at you," Dani challenged, starting down the stairs.

Libby clucked her tongue, jumping two steps to walk beside her. "You aren't supposed to threaten your bodyguard, Dani."

"I'm not threatening. I'm simply issuing a warning."

"How about a truce? I won't freeze your feet, and you won't shoot sparks at me?" Libby held out her hand.

"Deal." Dani shook it.

She hadn't given herself much time to stress about her Speed training, but now that it wasn't far off, the nerves were back in full force.

Over time, Dani had gotten used to her Sparker training sessions, eventually learning to appreciate the power because of them.

As enlightening as the Speed training sessions were sure to be, Dani doubted she'd ever appreciate speed the same way Amery did. He'd been obsessed with it since the day he manifested, using it every chance he got.

Dani had never wanted it in the first place.

It had taken her weeks to become fully comfortable with her sparks, and now, she could switch them out for whatever power she wanted whenever she wanted. It was exhilarating and terrifying all at once.

"Do you know if I'll be getting a new schedule from Sir Lechin?"

Sir Lechin was the closest thing Crystalium had to a school counselor, but he was also a Clairvoyant, a brytlyn with the very rare power to see the future in small doses. Sometimes, the magic was enough to make prophecies; most times, it wasn't.

Dani was still trying to figure out how Gernon Cryter had managed to foresee the one that had started this entire mess in the first place. She'd tried to ask The Golden Eagle about it once, and they had given the lackluster answer of "A Clairvoyant's power is difficult to understand if you don't have it."

But now, she could have it, couldn't she?

Still, what difference would it make if she did understand how a prophecy came to be? It wouldn't change anything about the one she'd been forced into.

It wouldn't change anything, really.

"You okay?" Libby asked, bringing Dani back to reality as they crossed the foyer. "You didn't say anything when I answered."

Dani blinked. "Sorry, what?"

Libby smiled patiently. "I said that you don't need to go see Sir Lechin because Headmistress Athena already took care of the schedule change, and both of your instructors have been informed."

"Was Madam Colette okay with it?"

"I guess so. She agreed to it, didn't she?" Libby shrugged. "But I'm not sure if Amery knows, so it'll be a fun surprise." She was practically bouncing with excitement.

"Sure." Dani sighed. "Fun."

"Okay. You go try to wolf down breakfast, and I'll go grab more snacks for later!" Libby told her, patting the satchel.

"More? That bag is full."

"You can never have too many snacks!"

"The session is only a few hours," Dani reminded her.

"And I've been looking forward to it for a day and a half. It's my number one source of entertainment from now on," Libby informed her.

"Please tell me you're joking!" Dani pleaded, watching as Libby spun around, headed for the kitchen.

Libby's only response was a laugh.

CHAPTER EIGHTEEN

Turns out, Amery did know about his new training mate and couldn't have been more ecstatic about the situation. He rambled on for almost the entirety of morning announcements about the Unstoppable Team Damery until Everett and Will pulled him back from the front row and Lydia put a hand over his mouth.

Because Thursdays were training days, their group split right after the Hall of Guidance, and Amery put it upon himself to serve as the tour guide.

"Where's Lieutenant Bower?" he asked as they weaved their way through the main hall of Crystalium, already a sea of blue uniforms.

Dani shrugged. "Libby said he's doing some security thing with my parents."

"For the Lirelight?" Amery wondered.

"Probably—wait, how do you know about that?" Dani hadn't told him about her upcoming party for a reason.

Amery grinned. "Will's been complaining about it."

"We're not excited," Dani confirmed.

"Why not?" Amery inquired. "Everyone showers you with presents, talks about how proud they are of you, and then there's lots of sweet treats. Sounds great to me."

"That's because you don't have to sit through a makeover," Dani muttered.

"I doubt that it'll be super drastic, Mystery. You're already perfect."

She snorted. "What do you know about makeovers?"

Amery arched an eyebrow. "Excuse me? I live with a girl who once spent three hours matching her lip gloss to hcr gown. The amount of times she's threatened to give me a makeover would appall you."

Lydia was the most fashion forward brytlyn Dani had ever met. She would probably be happiest getting her hair done and posing for dress fittings.

"She must be counting down the days until you two have one," Dani reasoned.

"Lyds can't wait." Amery sighed, rolling his eyes.

"You can?" Dani wondered, noticing his face bled dry of its usual enthusiasm.

Amery shook his head. "I don't want one."

"Really?" Dani narrowed her eyes. "Didn't you say that it sounded amazing?"

"Yeah, to attend, not to host," Amery corrected quickly.

"But you love attention!"

"Not when there's dancing involved, Mystery."

"You never dance at balls," Dani noted.

Amery smiled sympathetically. "It's a Lirelight tradition that the host or hosts dance first. It's mandatory."

"That's probably why Will's miserable," Dani realized. "He despises dancing."

"No, he's mad that he has to pick a partner."

Dani stopped in her tracks.

"Partner?"

Amery nodded, a pained expression on his face.
"You're not dancing with Will, Mystery. You have to pick a partner too."

Libby and Anders must've conveniently forgotten to fill her in on that.

Traitors.

"I do?" Callan had taught her to dance before the Winter Ball the year prior, but Dani hadn't done it since.

Amery waved his hand dismissively. "Don't worry, Mystery. I'm an incredible waltz partner."

Dani scoffed. "How do you know that I'm picking you?"

"Because I'm a better dancer than Everett and Eldridge are," he said, as if the very thought of her picking someone else was absurd.

"I've never seen you dance," Dani retorted.

"Well, I'm supremely talented; don't worry." Amery gave his most confident nod.

Dani rolled her eyes. "Of course you are."

"I am! I learned when I was little, and when I commit to something, I practice and practice until I get it. That's what's going to help me in the military academy."

"Military academy." Dani processed the words. "So, you want to be a soldier?"

Amery nodded.

"I want to be a general when I'm older—after I help you save the realm, of course. How else am I supposed to make a name for myself if I'm not your brilliant sidekick?"

"I still don't have a sidekick," Dani reminded him. Though it did shock her that Amery wanted to go to the military academy after graduation. Not that he wouldn't be a good soldier, just that she'd never pictured him doing anything like that.

She'd never given much thought to her life after Crystalium. Her only goal was to survive past her eighteenth birthday and stop a prophecy from killing her.

Anders had told her during her first day in Breckindale that she'd have the freedom to choose her future because she wasn't the next ruler of the realm. Just days later, the prophecy had been found, and that plan had been ruined.

"Whether you like it or not, I'm going to help you take down whoever's trying to destroy the realm," Amery said quietly, the determination setting his face aglow with excitement.

Dani knew that she needed to fill her friends in on everything. If the other boys and Lydia all reacted the same way as Amery, then The Golden Eagle was going to have a lot of medallions to prepare.

Sir Hugo's warning crept its way back to the forefront of her mind too, the foreboding truth that Amery didn't fully know what he was signing up for or what it would cost.

Dani chewed her lip, considering. "Okay." Amery wasn't going to take no for an answer anyway, and Dani did want his help.

Amery grinned, pumping his fist in victory. "And I get to make up my own codename."

"Why would you need a codename?" Dani wondered.

"Because every team uses codenames."

"We aren't exactly a team," Dani reminded him.

He frowned at her. "Mystery, do you really think that I'm the only one who wants in on this?"

"No," she answered honestly.

"Exactly, and wasn't the problem that Delacour went to her final battle alone?"

Dani deeply regretted telling them all about the previous chosen one.

"Yes."

"Precisely. So, in order to stop the prophecy from occurring, all we have to do is change things, make sure you do things better than she did. You can't do this alone, Glove Girl. You need backup, and you've got it. Not because you aren't good enough, but because you shouldn't have to be responsible for saving everyone alone. You're not Delacour, so why should you be her carbon copy?"

That might have been the nicest thing Amery had ever said to her.

"How long did you practice that speech?" Dani hoped her teasing could disguise the thickness in her throat.

"Wow, Mystery. That stings. That speech was custom made and spur of the moment." Amery put a hand on his heart, pausing for optimal dramatic effect before leading the way up the tower's winding staircase.

The higher they climbed, the more Dani gained a deeper contempt for tower stairs. Of course the room Amery used was at the very top. Dani was sure that if Anders had been with them, he would have offered to carry her when they reached the fifth flight.

Libby stayed silent as they walked, braiding her hair with one hand and holding the hilt of her sword with the other. She had an amazing habit of multitasking while also being ready to take on an army of assailants that made Dani very lucky to have her as a guard.

"You know, just to make you feel better about the whole Lirelight situation, I may just need to start brainstorming new nicknames for you," Amery decided, thrilled to share his brilliant idea.

"Like what?" Dani knew that this was Amery's way of trying to cheer her up. Humor was his coping mechanism, and it seemed to always work.

"How about The Great Glove Boss?" he suggested.

Dani snorted. "So original."

"Thank you, Glove Girl. I appreciate it."

Dani made sure he saw her roll her eyes before he knocked.

"You both can come in!"

Dani had been about to open the door when Amery grabbed her arm.

"Gloves," he whispered.

Dani had almost forgotten. "Thanks," she said gratefully, pulling off the royal blue gloves and reaching over to give them to Libby.

"When you need to use your speed, just give me a high five or something."

Dani nodded.

Amery nodded back and opened the door.

"Good morning, Madam Lexington!" Amery strode in, his confidence intact and smile ready. "Your star prodigy has arrived."

"Good morning, Amery." Madam Colette Lexington was a shorter woman with shoulder-length dark hair and eyes that lit up when she smiled. "And you must be Danielle."

"Yes, ma'am."

"Well, I'll admit it's uncommon to train two Speeds during one session, but considering the circumstances and the students, I am prepared to make an exception. I was told that after you manifested your speed, you injured yourself immediately, so that needs to be what we deal with first."

"Exactly. I think that I should have a free day, and you can help Mys—I mean Dani—learn how to use her power. It would be awful if she injured herself yet again." Amery turned up his charm, his infectious, excited grin endlessly bright.

Madam Colette was less than impressed. "You aren't having a free day. In fact, I think that this session will be very beneficial for both of you."

"Really?" His smile dropped.

"Of course. I think we often forget that the best way to improve our skills is through the example of others."

"You think I can learn from him?" Dani was sure that something must've been lost in translation.

Madam Colette nodded. "Yes, and I strongly believe that there is much that Amery can learn from you as well."

"I barely know what I'm doing," Dani admitted.

"That doesn't mean that you can't be a positive force," her new instructor encouraged.

"You are very inspirational," Amery agreed. "And as long as your rule following, do-good attitude doesn't run off on me, I think this will be a very helpful session."

"You hate learning," Dani objected.

"I hate learning boring subjects like history. I don't hate learning how to get better at super speed alongside my future wife," he corrected.

Dani would've slapped him if she was wearing her gloves. Instead, she settled for the best death glare ever given in the history of Breckindale.

Madam Colette already seemed to be fighting a headache.

"Be that as it may, I think it's best to start off with a few rules before we actually begin. First and most importantly, safety is the priority. Is that understood?"

She waited until they both nodded before continuing.

"Amery has already heard this lecture, but Danielle, you haven't, so I'll repeat it. Being a Speed is not dangerous, but without proper understanding and control, it can lead to danger, as you've already experienced. The goal isn't for you to be the fastest in the realm; it's for you to have the best understanding of both the power and its limits."

Dani thought that made sense. Sir Hugo had told her similar things when she'd first began her Sparker sessions.

Both Amery and Dani dutifully listened as Colette continued her lecture. It was mostly for Dani's benefit, though Amery seemed glad to hear it again too. Dani was surprised to see that he actually didn't argue or complain or even interrupt once, staying silent until their instructor finished and said, "Now, let's see what you can do, shall we?"

And when he did speak up, he turned to his new partner with a resolute nod. "Show her what you've got." Amery grinned, holding up his hand for a high five.

This time, Dani didn't leave him hanging. She did, however, wish she could absorb some of his confidence.

CHAPTER NINETEEN

"So, it went well?" Will asked as Amery and Dani made it to the table for lunch.

"I didn't crash, so yeah, I'd say so." Dani had siked herself out too much to use her full speed, but the circles she had raced around the training room had been fast and precise.

According to Madam Colette, her control was better than expected, which shocked Dani more than anyone else. She assumed that it had only been because her nerves had held her back. Amery's working theory was that because she'd absorbed the power from him for the second time, it was more stable.

Libby had wondered if that meant that Dani would continue to get stronger the more that she absorbed a brytlyn's power, but that experiment would need to be conducted in a controlled environment and most likely with Will, since reading minds didn't pose a big risk.

"More importantly, she didn't lose control, and we kept the secret until the gloves came back on. I think I deserve a round of applause for my efforts as the personal assistant to the most powerful brytlyn ever," Amery declared, awaiting his praise.

He didn't receive any.

Lydia rolled her eyes at her twin before turning back to Dani. "But that's great, right? Didn't it take you a lot longer to do this with your sparks?"

"Yeah, and I think it may have to do with my absorption." Dani filled them all in on Amery's theory, expecting at least one of her friends to tell her that she was crazy and find a magical loophole that further proved she didn't know as much about Breckindale as she needed to.

No one did.

"That … actually would make sense," Eldridge told her. "If you absorb a power, you'd also be absorbing the necessary skills to be good at using it. Since you've already tapped into Amery's power, it would be easier than absorbing a new one."

"So, the more you absorb, the better you'll get?" Lydia frowned In confusion, trying to connect the dots.

"I'm not totally sure," Dani said. "It's only a guess, and as far as we know, it might only be a Speed thing. Besides, I definitely need training if I'm going to get good at this absorbing thing, and this could just mean that I'm not set up to fail."

"Manifesting is never random," Will disagreed. "There's no way that you'd get a power that would mess things up completely, even if your magic works differently than ours."

It was true. Being the Savior meant a lot more than just having to save the realm and deal with a prophecy trying to kill her; it meant that she had more magic inside her than any other brytlyn.

It was a blessing and a curse that Dani was still struggling to accept.

Her magic was the reason she'd only gotten to Breckindale months before. It was the reason her entire life was messed up beyond repair until she either died or saved herself from that fate.

"You're probably right." It was hard not to wish the prophecy had made a mistake and chosen the wrong person for the job. That type of denial sometimes took the edge off of the terror that her nightmares fed on every night, but it never lasted. It couldn't. There was absolutely nothing that Dani could do to change the prophecy.

On one hand, it was awesome to know that she could do so much with one power.

But on the other hand, she didn't want to be able to do anything either. Taking off her gloves could mean an accident, and she couldn't risk that, especially not with Iris already out for blood.

"So, how goes the Lirelight planning?" Everett grinned knowingly.

Will slumped over and rested his face on the table. Whether in protest or in answer, Dani couldn't be sure. Knowing her brother, it was probably both.

"I've been told that we can't cancel it or suspiciously get injured or sick," Dani shared.

"And that's why we didn't want one," Everett declared.

"Oh, hush it, Ev," Lydia complained, leaning over the table in excitement, bright smile intact. "Okay, so what's the look?"

"The look?" Dani only gave her a blank stare in return.

"Your new look for the Lirelight," Lydia prompted, finally taking pity on her best friend and continuing, "You haven't met with a stylist yet?"

"Oh, that look. No, I haven't met with a stylist yet." And Dani was dreading when she'd have to.

Lydia folded her hands on the table. "I want to be the first to see the gown."

Dani had fully expected that. "You will, I promise. If you want, you can even come when I have fittings. You're a lot better at this than I am."

Lydia beamed. "Of course, and I have some ideas already on color schemes."

Dani really shouldn't have been surprised. In addition to being an absolute genius, Lydia was also a fantastic artist, and the sketches displayed all over her room were stunningly detailed.

"You and Libby should have a full conversation about it. I've never seen her so excited about something."

"Oh, I can't wait for your Lirelight," Libby agreed, appearing behind Dani. "Sorry, I thought you heard me walking over."

"Lydia has ideas for my stylist," Dani informed her guard.

Libby nodded approvingly. "And this is why Lydia is my favorite."

"Excuse me!"

Libby winked. "You're great too, Amery. Very entertaining."

"Thank you," Amery said.

Libby narrowed her eyes. "Do I want to know why Will's asleep?"

"He's dealing with the emotional toll a Lirelight takes on you," Eldridge explained.

Everett tried to snatch his cookie, and Will smacked his hand away. "And he's definitely not sleeping."

"Yeah, I remember the feeling all too well."

"You dreaded yours too?" Dani had figured Libby had thrived with all of the demands a Lirelight involved. Except for her hair, she'd said nothing but positive things about the party.

"I wasn't always such a big fan of attention," Libby revealed.

Dani found that really hard to believe.

"Seriously?"

"I used to be the shyest brytlyn ever," Libby admitted. "And I despised dancing with a burning passion."

Eldridge snorted. "All of us do. Dancing is the worst."

"The worst!" Will echoed, his words muffled against the table surface.

Dani nodded, shuddering. "Speaking of dancing, why didn't you tell me about the dancing tradition in this lovely little celebration?"

"Because I knew that you'd hate it." Libby shrugged.

"Do I really have to dance in front of all of the guests?" Dani complained, hoping that maybe there was still a chance Amery had been kidding.

Libby crushed her dreams with a nod. "Yep, all four hundred and seventy-nine of them."

"Four hundred and seventy-nine!" Both Will and Dani practically shouted the number.

"That's just the amount of invitations being sent out," Libby promised, obviously not understanding Dani's horrified expression.

"We usually don't have that many people," Will argued.

Libby gave them a pitying look. "Yeah, but this is a Lirelight."

"It's important, I know," Dani gritted out.

Libby offered an encouraging smile. "You worry too much. You'll be fine and it'll be fun."

"Yeah, for you," Dani muttered.

"It'll be a night you'll remember forever."

"Yeah, for you."

"You know, you two really do sound like sisters sometimes." Will sat up finally, a red mark on his forehead the only evidence of his slump.

"You are kinda proving his point with your matching glares," Amery agreed.

Libby was not amused.

"You do realize that if I was your older sister, Will, I could ground you and lock you in the library, right?"

"Point taken," Will surrendered.

"I don't think big sisters are supposed to give so many threats," Amery muttered.

Everett shook his head. "You don't have one."

"That's fair."

Dani frowned at Libby. "Do I honestly have to pick someone to dance with?"

"I was wondering when you'd complain about that." Libby was enjoying her misery way too much. "And yes, you do."

"Libby!"

"Don't look at me like that. I don't make the rules. I'm just the innocent messenger here."

"The innocent messenger who's finding joy from forcing me to play dress up," Dani hissed.

"You'll have fun, I promise."

"I doubt it," Will grumbled.

"If there were cameras here, you would definitely be videoing this whole thing," Dani muttered miserably.

Libby frowned. "I don't know what that means, so I'm just going to assume you're right. And there will be portraits of both of you and your family taken."

"That's not so bad." Lydia at least tried to stay on the bright side.

"Yeah, if you don't mind staying still for a while. Remember when mom forced us to sit for one a few years ago?" Eldridge asked Everett.

"I blocked it out," he replied.

Amery clutched his head. "Okay, enough Lirelight talk. It's

depressing me."

"You don't have yours for a while," Will told Amery.

"And I'm still dreading it!"

"Hey, do you guys want to come to Elthorne after school?" Dani had a feeling that her explanation would take a lot longer than just lunch to explain, and a subject change was definitely needed.

"Sure," Lydia said as the others nodded their agreement. It wasn't weird for all of them to come to Elthorne, but Dani usually wasn't the one to invite them.

This time, it was important.
This time, she was finally going to tell her friends the truth … and hope that they didn't hate her.

That thought took up her brain for the remainder of the day.

Dani spent her physical education session switching between excitement and nerves about finally including her friends in her biggest secret yet, and it lasted until she made it home and was stopped in the foyer with her brother by Giselle, Grennet, and Ronan.

A guard whispered something to Anders and he headed up the stairs abruptly, scaring Dani even more than the looks the Magicals wore.

Anders had used his speed.

Another guard said something to both Libby and Leo in a low tone, and they headed upstairs too.

"What's going on?" Dani finally asked.

Will and Giselle made eye contact for a second, and Will's face went pale.

"Something bad," she deduced.

Grennet straightened, exchanging a look with Giselle and Ronan. "The Queen is dying."

CHAPTER TWENTY

Dani had already paced twenty laps in her brother's room by the time Anders eventually returned. No other guards were with him.

"Anything?" Will was perched on the edge of his bed, throwing a triangular ball in the air and catching it for the umpteenth time.

It was the first word he'd spoken since they'd made it upstairs. Neither had wanted to be alone, and their unspoken solution had been Will's room.

"She is still unconscious, but Cornelius is doing all he can," Anders informed them.

Dani was sure that he was.

"When can we see her?" Dani questioned.

Anders must've been anticipating the question. "Now, if you'd like, but you should be warned that she doesn't look well."

Will jumped up. "Has he figured out what's wrong?"

"Your father will explain," Anders answered, and for once, Dani understood why he never let his emotions show. He had to be the strong one in every situation, even and especially when others weren't.

Dani hadn't taken off her gloves in fear of letting her sparks loose, but now, she wished that she had. Holding everything in was a lot harder.

The walk to the King and Queen's wing was familiar, but this time, Dani and Will weren't going to prank their parents or fill them in on their school days.

Every guard they passed had their head bowed, like they were silently paying their respects. It made Dani want to walk the other way.

I don't want to go in there. Is that bad?

It wasn't common for Will to transfer messages into Dani's mind, but when he did do it, it was always perfectly clear.

No; I don't want to either.

But they both would. Because their mom was dying.

Dani didn't want to think much about that. She'd spent weeks trying to get into her mother's head and understand how she'd been able to be an operative for The Golden Eagle for thirteen years while ruling a realm and keeping it a secret from everyone.

Dani hadn't been able to figure it out, but she did conclude that her mother was one of the most incredible brytlyns ever, and even though she initially was upset about it, Amandine being a part of The Golden Eagle made her feel a little bit less alone. She didn't want to lose that.

She just wanted to pretend it wasn't real … which became really hard once they made it just outside the King and Queen's bedroom and saw the Magicals standing outside the closed door.

Dani grabbed her brother's hand as Giselle opened the door and steered them in. Seeing her father slumped beside the bed was enough to make tears fill her eyes, but one glance at her mother made both her and Will squeeze each other's hands. Hard.

Amandine's skin was so pale it was practically translucent, her usually rosy cheeks and red lips were gray, and she looked at least twenty years older.

Callan looked up just as the twins joined him on her left side. "Hey, guys." He looked exhausted, mentally more than physically, and desperately needed good news. Dani hugged him.

"When did it happen?" Will asked, his voice thick.

Her father could hardly speak. "This morning. She was perfectly fine until an hour after breakfast when she said that she was going to rest, and when I went to check on her, she was like this."

"Cornelius is going to save her, isn't he?" Dani only asked the question because she was betting on one answer, the only answer that was acceptable.

"I'm working on it," Cornelius promised, walking in with a satchel full of vials. "That's why I said that you two could come visit. Amandine is no longer in critical condition."

Dani hadn't smiled wider all day.

"Really?" Will's eyes practically lit up with hope.

Callan nodded. "Cornelius managed to stabilize her, so as long as she gets doses during the night and then twice a day, she'll make it for a few more days."

The smiles dropped.

"That's it?" Dani was trying to stay positive, but she'd been hoping for something more concrete, like an estimate of when her mother would be fully recovered.

"Until she wakes up," Cornelius agreed.

"When will that be?" Will wanted to know.

"We don't know," Callan admitted.

Dani's heart sank. "That potion won't make her better?"

"I still haven't been able to figure out what caused this," Cornelius said, fishing through his satchel. "Right now, all I can do is stabilize her condition and make sure it doesn't spread."

"So, Mom's going to stay like that for a while?" Dani tried to focus on the bright side. Asleep was better than dead.

Their father gave a solemn nod. "For now."

"I'm hoping that it will be sooner rather than later. If it's poison, then I know how I can save her, but until I get to the cause, then all I can do is give her this." Cornelius held up a violet-colored potion. "Unfortunately, to make more, I'll need a Revere Root, and I don't have any more."

"What happens if you run out without it?" Will asked.

"The Queen dies."

"I'll send a team to retrieve it at once," Callan promised, somehow managing to be more determined than Dani had ever seen.

"The Revere Root grows at the very edge of the Northern Forest. We both know that a simple team may not suffice," Cornelius warned.

Dani and Will exchanged a look. The Northern Forest was a notoriously dangerous part of Breckindale, and it hadn't been inhabited by brytlyns in hundreds of years. It was guarded by dangers even the noblest of guards didn't dare cross.

The Magicals must've been eavesdropping or spending time practicing walking in a formation because they chose that moment to enter in a surprisingly neat fashion before Edon spoke.

"They'll need to be powerful, have good knowledge of the realm and its terrain, and know brytlyn skills and be able to wield them effectively. You need a team who is used to cutting things close and has no fear."

Dani was used to tuning the Magicals out at times when they decided to rant or give long speeches, but this one gave her an idea. A brilliant idea. A brilliantly stupid idea that would probably get shot down but was worth a try anyway. One look at her brother proved they he knew exactly what she was thinking, and his nod told her to share it.

"We'll go," Dani spoke up.

"What?" The Magicals hadn't been expecting that evidently, as they spoke as one.

Dani cleared her throat, standing taller. "Will and I would like to go."

"Absolutely not!" Callan thundered. "I'm not going to lose you two."

"You won't, Dad. I actually think I know some people who can help with this."

"Who?" Arabella asked calmly.

Dani bit her lip. "I can't tell you." Technically, she wasn't supposed to bring them up at all, but they were her best bet at knowing something helpful. Besides, they would want to help her mom too.

Iris rolled her eyes impatiently.

"How is this helpful if you won't tell us anything?"

"You'll just have to trust me," Dani insisted.

Iris laughed, sugary and fake and brushing Dani off. "I'm sorry—the Queen's life is on the line and you want to consider the opinion of a teenager who has only been in the realm for a few months?"

"I'm the most powerful brytlyn in existence. I have a better chance than any guard, even Anders," Dani challenged.

Giselle nodded from behind Iris. Clearly, Dani had played her cards well.

As always, Iris wasn't about to be outvoted, especially by the princess.

"What about the Crown Prince? Surely, we aren't sending the future of the monarchy into a dangerous quest."

"If Dani goes, then I go," Will said, his expression daring anyone to question him. Dani grinned confidently.

"And no doubt you'll want the Callisto and Varron children to come along on this trip as well." Edon narrowed his eyes, considering.

"Actually, that's a pretty good idea," Will decided.

"They'd want to come," Dani agreed.

"Sending six children out into the wild is not the safest or preeminent option. Yes, Dani has a strong chance, especially with both of her powers, but she'd need other brytlyns to absorb, and five reasonably untrained ones are not ideal candidates," Cordelia argued.

"Amery's really amazing with his speed, and I've absorbed his power twice now." Dani couldn't believe she was complimenting him. "Eldridge has good control with his light, and Lydia can change her appearance whenever she wants."

"What about Will and the other Callisto?" Milos narrowed his eyes at the twins.

"Will can be in charge of communication, and Everett can read emotions to gauge threats if we run into someone or something while we're there."

"And we're both top of our class in physical education," Will promised. "Our friends are not far behind either."

Dani nodded. "Reasonably untrained may be an understatement here."

Callan bristled, his expression uncompromising. "I still don't think this is a good idea."

"At least consider it, Dad," Dani pleaded. "You don't have to send a team out until tomorrow."

Callan shook his head firmly. "Neither of you are going."

"But—"

"Favian and Genevieve are coming over to help with things, and I already made arrangements for you two to spend the night with the Varrons. Everett and Eldridge will be heading over too since Bree is at a friend's house. We can discuss this at another time."

"Fine." Dani wasn't about to argue, not when she knew she wouldn't win.

She was, however, going to pack the golden medallion hidden under her mattress.

CHAPTER TWENTY-ONE

"Worst. Sleepover. Ever." Lydia emphasized every word with a loud sigh.

Everett shot her a wry smile. "You're just saying that because it's too late to do anything fun."

"And because we were forced into it." Eldridge was perched on the arm of the sofa, book in hand.

Everett nodded. "That too."

"If it helps," Will offered, "we did nominate you to go on a really dangerous adventure."

Lydia perked up. "Where?"

"The Northern Forest."

"That would be dangerous," Eldridge considered.

Amery grinned. "And awesome. Don't forget awesome."

"Why are people going to the Northern Forest in the first place?" Lydia asked.

"To get a Revere Root," Dani explained. "My mom won't last much longer without it."

Everett cleared his throat. "We're really sorry about that, by the way. I know we haven't said it yet."

Will gave a hint of a smile. "Thanks."

"I want to go to the Northern Forest!" Amery announced, standing up eagerly. "Just to prove that someone can do it and get home without nearly dying."

"My dad won't agree to it. He hated the idea." Dani sighed.

Lydia threw her arms up.
"Obviously! It's supposed to be nearly impossible."

"But regular guards won't stand a chance, and if someone doesnt get Revere Root, then our mom dies." And Dani couldn't bring herself to picture a reality where Amandine didn't exist.

"So, we go," Eldridge decided. "All of us. If we're the best brytlyns for the job, then we should do it."

Lydia narrowed her eyes. "So, we get to miss school *and* go on an adventure?"

Dani nodded.

"I'm in," Amery and Everett said together.

Dani pulled at her gloved fingers nervously. "Before you guys make any decisions, there is something that you all should know—a lot of things, actually."

"Okay." Amery frowned. "What's up, Mystery?"

"You guys have to promise that you won't share this with anyone, though. I'm not supposed to tell any brytlyn at all."

"We promise." Will didn't know where this was going either, but he agreed without a second thought.

Dani blew out a breath she hadn't realized she'd been holding. "First off, I should probably say that I'm really, really sorry that I didn't tell you all sooner, but I technically wasn't allowed to, so it's also not my fault."

There was no easy way to admit all of her secrets, but Dani had a habit of rambling when she was sharing things, and this time was no different.

And she did, sharing everything from The Golden Eagle's history with Delacour to what really happened when she blinked after the ball, Sir Hugo's training and war sessions, her golden-costumed council, and finally the Midnight Dragon. She was honest, more honest than she probably should have been, but they deserved to know everything, and so Dani made sure they did. She even told them about Amandine, making sure her brother read her thoughts first so he could be the first to know. He took it better than she expected, though it may have been because Dani explained how The Golden Eagle could help.

Dani waited for them to respond, certainly not expecting the first words to be from the Lord of Hindley himself.

"This is why you're so mysterious," Amery said, his voice sounding far more calm than the gobsmacked expression on his face.

"Guess so." Dani let out an uneasy laugh. "Any questions about this stuff?"

"I have a question!" Will spoke up.

"Go ahead," Dani encouraged.

"How do we join?"

Dani walked over to where she'd set down her bag and fished her golden medallion out. No guards had come with Dani or Will because they were all necessary for the palace lockdown. She couldn't get in trouble for ditching Anders if he had ditched her first.

She held it up. "This can take us to their main base, and I think I can convince my council to allow you guys to become members if you want to."

"Well, you already know that I'm in," Amery assured her, glancing around at the other five.

"Me too," Will agreed, just as quick as Dani figured he would offer.

Everett said, "Sounds fun," only a split second before Eldridge followed with, "Let's do it."

"Lydia?" Amery turned to his twin.

"I'm the official best friend of the most powerful brytlyn ever born. Why wouldn't I want to be a part of this?"

"You guys are seriously amazing, but this means that no one can know about any of this. It means lying to your family and other friends and being involved in a really dangerous war, plus sneaking out of your houses late very frequently to do this."

"Did we or did we not talk about this earlier, Mystery?" Amery started.

"We didn't talk about what a ginormous decision this is," Dani argued.

"Well, we are all still in."

"You can't speak for everyone," she warned him.

Amery crossed his arms, turning away from her to face the other occupants of the room instead. "Will?" he asked.

The Crown Prince of Breckindale waited for the others to nod before answering.

"We're in."

"Okay, then." Dani adjusted her grip on the medallion so that her thumb rested just above the frost crystal. "Everyone has to hold hands for this one." Dani didn't hear even one grumble as Amery took her right and Will her left, and the chain formed from there.

"Are you sure your parents won't come check on us?" Eldridge brought up a very good point.

"Mom falls asleep and is dead to the world. Dad stays up, but he usually reads. We'll be fine," Lydia promised.

"Ready, then?"

Once she got six nods, Dani pressed the crystal and they blinked away.

She barely reacted when the group landed in the blue forest of Frovland; her friends … not so much.

It took her a moment to realize that none of them had ever been outside their realm before. Dani had been in shock her first time too.

"So, this is the East Entrance of Frovland?" Will asked, looking around at the frigid blue surroundings.

"Not what you expected?" Dani felt her lips twitch into a proud smile.

To be fair, the riddle hadn't given anything else to go on but the name of the location.

"I thought you said there was a base here." Lydia frowned, going over to stand beside her brother.

"There is," Dani promised. "You guys should probably step back before I give the signal."

Eldridge frowned. "Signal?"

"Blitzspire is underground."

Dani realized that she probably should have offered a better explanation for what was about to happen a second after she cupped a hand near her mouth and shouted, "I'm here!" into the trees, but the molten metal dropped from the sky and the whirlpool formed and she lost time.

"Would you guys prefer to fall or jump?"

Her usually fearless friends stayed silent. Far more silent than Dani had ever witnessed them being.

"It can't hurt you, I promise," she said. "It just feels like a huge blast of wind for a few seconds and then you land."

"I'll go first," Eldridge offered, giving a confident nod and jumping in on shaky legs.

His bravery seemed to urge the others on, with Everett, Will, and Lydia jumping one after the other until only Amery and Dani were left above ground.

"Don't tell me the Great Amery Varron is scared."

"I'm not scared," he promised, lying through his teeth. "See you on the other side, Mystery." And then he did a cannonball and disappeared from sight.

Dani gave herself a moment to collect herself and then jumped too, landing in a perfected crouch that had taken her a solid three months to master.

"Don't worry; someone will come to get us soon," she promised, noticing both the awe and confusion on her friends' faces. "By the way, everyone here will be wearing gold cloaks, so you won't see what they really look like. The only brytlyn here who isn't in disguise is Sir Hugo."

"You weren't kidding?" Everett asked.

Dani snorted. "Nope, this is actually my life."

"And you don't find that creepy?" Lydia wondered.

Dani shrugged. "You get used to it."

"Do you really do this every night?" Will questioned.

"Pretty much."

"No wonder you're always exhausted."

"I do try to sleep; it just doesn't like me very much," Dani mumbled.

Eldridge raised his hand. "Sorry. Just to recap here: We just blinked to a different realm, got swallowed up by a magic whirlpool, and now are in the holding room of a secret organization that is run by a bunch of brytlyns in gold and the teenage chosen one?"

"Yep," Dani agreed. "Though it sounds a lot crazier when you put it like that."

"Did you tell them that we were coming?" Will looked around frantically, like an operative would pop up randomly behind them.

"No, but I'm sure they realized." Dani looked around, half expecting to find a hidden camera or something embedded in one of the sleek walls. Human technology was more or less non-existent in Breckindale, but she still checked.

The front wall began to move, and Dani was expecting one of her council members to appear in all of their gold finery and give some dramatic greeting to her friends … or maybe scold her for blinking the entire group to the base without actually giving a proper warning.

But when the tunnel opened up, the person on the other side wasn't Radian, Nova, Tobin, or Scala. It was just a brytlyn in a golden cloak.

"Is this one of your advisors?" Lydia's expression twisted into confusion.

"No." Dani had never seen any members of her council wearing a cloak. "I think it's just one of the members."

Dani had met a handful of Golden Eagle operatives, but none of them had ever offered anything more than a code name. The only face that Dani ever saw was her mother's or Sir Hugo's.

Which was why Dani found it so surprising when the figure pulled back her hood to reveal a tall Asian woman with long, jet black hair.

"My name is Ivy," the woman said, her blue eyes piercing with a precise gaze. "I'm your handler."

CHAPTER TWENTY-TWO

"Handler?" Dani repeated, eyes narrowed at the woman in front of her.

"I am in charge of you and your friends while you're at any Golden Eagle base," Ivy clarified.

"So, like a bodyguard?"

"Or a babysitter," Amery muttered.

"Yes and no. Officially, I'm in charge of keeping you all safe and out of trouble while you are under the protection of The Golden Eagle."

"Why now?" Dani questioned.

"Because you've proven yourself very capable on your own," Ivy answered, her compliment severely lacking warmth. "And you already have plenty of security. Your friends don't."

"So, our membership is already approved?" Will guessed.

Ivy promptly spun on her heel. "You'll have to talk with the council about that. I'm supposed to escort you all there now."

Dani followed her, glancing back as her friends took in their silver surroundings.

"So, if we need anything, we go to you?" Everett wondered.

"That's how it's going to work," Ivy agreed. "Obviously, you'll always go to Dani first, but after that, it should be me."

Their new handler rapped on the door and opened it after three seconds.

"Are you a part of the council now?" Dani asked Ivy when she entered.

Ivy shook her head. "I'm not supposed to let any of you out of my sight."

Anders and Libby had never been allowed in.

Dani normally would have gone to her usual place at the end of the table, but this time, she made it halfway to the center and waited for her friends.

"You weren't kidding about the gold," Amery muttered out of the side of his mouth.

Dani shook her head. "Guys, meet Sir Hugo, Nova, Tobin, Scala, and Radian. They're my council."

"Council, this is Amery, Everett, Lydia, Will, and Eldridge, the brilliant teenagers who solved your riddle all on their own."

The glimmer of pride made her smile slightly as she faced The Golden Eagle. Her friends were capable and smart and incredibly talented all on their own.
Dani had been the weak one, hiding in her room after having a fight with her parents and some of the Magicals for hiding the scroll Giselle had given her.

The five of them had investigated, scoured dozens of books about codes both brytlyn and human codes to solve the one that would lead to The Golden Eagle.

"It is a privilege to meet you all." Sir Hugo nodded his head respectfully. "We have all heard quite a bit about each of you."

"So, Mystery does brag about us." Amery seemed to be the only one not shell-shocked, elbowing Dani.

"Crazy, right?" Dani retorted.

"Dani speaks very highly of you—all of you," Radian assured them, resting his armored hands on the table. "Which is part of why we've agreed to extend our membership."

"What's the other part?" Eldridge wanted to know.

"In light of recent developments, a new approach may be a strength that our organization needs. Provided that you allow Ivy to do her job and heed the advice of Dani's bodyguards, a select team of teenagers could very well be an asset."

Amery's eyes lit up. "So, what do we get to do?"

Will grinned for the first time since they'd arrived. "And do they involve secret passageways?"

"Or spying?" Everett chimed in.

"They involve staying out of all dangers possible." Ivy shut them down.

"If there is an opportunity for a suitable assignment, then it will be brought to Ivy, and she will decide the terms of your involvement," Sir Hugo told them, the seriousness of his expression dissuading any arguments.

"Would going to the Northern Forest count as a suitable assignment?" Dani questioned.

"Why would you go to the Northern Forest?" Scala asked.

At first, Dani was surprised, but then she realized that the only person who would be updating them about things at the palace was the reason for the quest in the first place.

"Our mom is sick. If we want her to live longer than a few days, we need a plant from the Northern Forest," Will answered.

"We will assist in every way that we can," Sir Hugo promised.

Dani smiled gratefully. "Thank you."

"We can send a small team of operatives to the Northern Forest and retrieve it for you." Ivy offered the kindest words she'd spoken so far.

"Actually, one is already assembled," Amery said instead.

"Who?" Radian stared directly at Dani.

"Us," the six said together.

"Pardon?" Sir Hugo narrowed his eyes.

Dani stood up straighter. "The team needs to be powerful and have certain skills in order to succeed."

"And you all possess those qualities." Radian didn't make the question an accusation, simply stating a valid concern.

"According to our leader." Amery nodded toward Dani.

"You believe that this arrangement will work?"

"I don't know," Dani admitted truthfully. "It could."

"Do Anders and Libby know that you're doing this?" Scala asked.

"No." Libby might see the fun adventure side of it, but there was absolutely no possible way that Anders would ever let her go.

"But just hear me out here, okay? The Northern Forest isn't easy to get through, and even the best guards have weaknesses."

"So do six teenagers," Tobin argued.

"Who spend more time training with our magic than any adults up for the job. We know how and when to use our skills and all have a good understanding of our powers," Dani challenged.

"You're all supremely talented," Sir Hugo conceded. "Nevertheless, this journey is not one meant to be endured by children."

"If I'm supposed to end a war in a few months, I'm pretty sure I can handle this."

Sir Hugo blew out a long, tired sigh. "I'll admit, your plan isn't necessarily a flawed one, and you do have valid points, but I cannot imagine the king will not notice your absence."

"He's against it, but no decision has been made yet," Will explained.

Dani went straight to the point before her council could shut her down completely. "We're going whether or not he agrees. Is there anything I need to do or know to save my mom?"

"We will, of course, offer anything that we can to ensure you succeed. Extra operatives as backups, supplies that may assist, and if you do, indeed, plan to do this, then Ivy will be accompanying you," Nova answered.

All heads turned to the dark-haired woman who was nodding silently, her expression betraying no hint of emotion.

"Thank you," Dani told her council before turning around to Ivy and telling her the same thing. She was risking her life for kids that she didn't know, after all.

"I suppose it is as good a time as any to introduce you to Ember," Radian abruptly announced.

"Ember?"

Sir Hugo nodded. "Delacour had a dragon when she was your age that assisted with organization affairs and missions. Delacour planned for you to have her descendant, and Flame's granddaughter, Ember, has been training for the past three years."

"Dani gets a dragon?" If Lydia's jaw dropped any farther, it would have hit the ground.

"She does indeed," Tobin said.

"Would you like to meet her?" Scala asked.

Dani nodded. "Sure."

A flash of light made Dani's vision fill with dark spots, refocusing to reveal a silver creature that barely fit in the room without ducking her head low. Ember appeared completely calm while the six teenagers jumped back, cheered in excitement, and then stood frozen in terror and wonder.

Dani eventually unfroze enough to take a few steps closer, one hand out just in case the creature got spooked. It wasn't necessary, of course, because the dragon nuzzled her hand instead before dipping into a surprisingly elegant bow.

Dani froze again.

Her friends, of course, had no fear at all. They respectfully waited for Dani to greet Ember first before petting her gently themselves and remarking how awesome she was. Ember seemed to love the attention and, in addition to bonding with her owner, appeared to adore each of the other excited brytlyns.

The council and Ivy hung back for a few more minutes before moving to Dani's side.

"This was supposed to be an early birthday present," Nova whispered.

Dani turned to face her, nearly stepping on her advisor's golden gown. "From you guys?"

Her council had never given her anything before, unless a medallion and some advice counted. She was about to consider the possibility of the gift being from Delacour, but Nova beat her to it.

"From Amandine."

Dani nodded, afraid that if she spoke, she'd break down.

"Dragons, as I am sure you've all learned in school, can sense danger and also blink with astounding accuracy. Now that Ember is familiar with your scent, Dani, she will be able to sense danger and blink to you. All of you."

"Dragon backup … cool," Everett breathed.

"If I knew that you got to meet dragons here, I would have wanted to be a member of your organization a lot earlier," Will said.

"I'm glad you said that because there is still one more test that you five must complete to officially gain membership," Tobin told them.

"Really?" Dani hadn't known that.

"Well, whatever it is, bring it on," Amery vowed resolutely. "We're all in."

Dani had to smile.

Sir Hugo nodded, though he looked unsurprised. "Well, then, Ivy, would you mind grabbing the devices, please? We should begin having you all swear your oaths."

Ivy nodded and stepped out of the secret door hidden along one of the walls. It was the same door Amandine had used when she'd revealed herself to Dani.

"Did you swear an oath?" Lydia asked, interrupting the memory.

Dani shook her head. "I was just accepted."

"She's the heir to the organization, and that requires no oath of allegiance. Though she did have a choice to accept her leadership role," Radian explained.

That part was true.

"Do they get medallions too?" Dani wondered.

"We should have them ready by tomorrow evening," Scala confirmed.

Ivy returned, five golden spheres in her hands. "They'll only flash green if you are completely honest."

"So, they're lie detectors?" Dani realized.

"I suppose that's one way to think of them. Every member has to hold one of these while they complete their path to ensure their loyalties lie in helping the realm, not harming," Sir Hugo explained.

"Do you seriously think they want to hurt the realm?"

"It's protocol."

"Got it." Dani stepped slightly away from the group, not wanting to get in the way of whatever was going to happen.

"Actually, Dani, you'll be administering the oaths." Scala stopped her.

"Why?"

"Because they are swearing their allegiance to you." Tobin sounded confused by the question altogether.

"I don't want to be their leader," Dani objected quickly.

"Maybe not," Sir Hugo continued, "but The Golden Eagle was founded to assist you in protecting and defending the realm from all harm."

"I've never done this before."

"You haven't needed to."

Dani folded her arms but didn't argue. "What do I do?"

"Take their hand and copy my words," Sir Hugo answered.

Will volunteered to go first, and Dani was grateful.

Ivy put the golden sphere in his right hand, and Dani took his left.

"I will protect," Sir Hugo told her quietly.

"I will protect," Dani told Will, who repeated the phrase with a kind of gravity and reverence that made her sure that he'd be a good king.

"I will defend."

"I will defend," Will promised.

"I will fight alongside the Savior for justice and peace." Dani nearly tripped over her own title, the weight of the oath hitting her deeply as her brother recited the words with absolute certainty.

The last part was easier, but still heavy.

"And I will strive to always protect the realm and its people no matter the circumstances."

Will passed with flying colors, the orb flashing green almost immediately after he'd spoken the last word. Eldridge, Amery, and Lydia finished with similar results, none intimidated by the gravity of the words or the promises they'd made.

Dani was, and she wasn't even the one being judged.

"Congratulations," Sir Hugo told them when Everett had finished, orb flashing green. "You are all members of The Golden Eagle."

CHAPTER TWENTY-THREE

"So, we all know the plan?"

"Yeah, we need to all be in agreement for this."

"No shutting down, no backing out."

"We got it. Just make sure that we all get back here in twenty minutes. Understood?"

"Yes, ma'am."

It had been decided that leaving that night would be easiest and give them the best opportunity to slip away.

Dani and Will would return to Elthorne to pack the supplies that they needed while the Callisto twins would do the same at Umbergrove. Amery and Lydia were in charge of securing gemstones for blinking and maps from Greenaway House's library, which they had blinked to from Blitzspire only a few minutes before. Once done, they would all be meeting back at Umbergrove and using Dani's pendant to go to Frovland, where Ivy would be waiting.

The forest itself was notoriously risky to blink into, but the surrounding terrain wasn't. As long as they were able to pinpoint an exact location, the first part of the quest would be a piece of cake.

"See you guys soon." Will held out a gem to Dani, and she passed two to Everett and Eldridge.

"You got it." Amery nodded, and both sets of twins blinked away and back to their respective homes. Umbergrove was empty, but Elthone… Well, Elthorne was the exact opposite, completely packed with brytlyns, all of whom would alert Callan the second his twins were spotted.

Fortunately, there was a secret passage on the side of the estate that would lead inside, and Will knew it like the back of his hand.

They snuck in easily enough, even managing to make it up the stairs unnoticed, only thanks to how dark the palace was at night and the lack of guards stationed in the foyer. The twins had spotted more outside than usual. By utilizing even more secret passageways and deserted hallways, they made it to their wing both ahead of schedule and without alerting anyone of their presence.

"Where do you two think you're going?" a voice hissed, appearing out of the shadows two feet from Dani's bedroom.

"Libby?" Dani recognized the puffy pink tunic even in the dark. "What are you doing?"

"Following orders. What are you doing?"

"I forgot my backpack," Dani told her.

Libby raised a brow. "And you're coming to get it at midnight?"

"Yes," Will answered far too quickly.

Libby made no move to even pretend that she believed them.

"What are you two really doing here? Before you answer, remember that I'm obligated to alert my superior guard of any disturbance."

"Anders is your superior." Dani's jaw tightened at the realization.

"Exactly." Libby grinned.

Dani sighed. As soon as Anders knew his charge was here, she'd either be on the other side of a lecture or have to personally deal with an overprotective bodyguard.

"Will you freak out if I tell you the truth?"

Libby shrugged. "Probably not."

"But you can't tell anyone about this," Dani warned.

"Fine."

"We're going to the Northern Forest tonight."

Libby blinked, the words registering in her brain. "I'm sorry, you're what?"

"Going to save Mom," Will added hastily.

Dani nodded insistently. "The Golden Eagle is helping us, and we have a plan."

"I'm going too," Libby declared, which Dani probably should've expected.

"Don't you have to stay here and be a guard?" Will wondered.

"Technically, my job is still to protect your sister, so I'm not doing anything wrong by leaving. You two go pack."

"Okay." Dani, in truth, was very grateful that Libby was coming with them, not least because she would make things fun. "Libby, would you mind going to get us gems?"

"How many do you need?"

"A dozen or so." Will peeked his head out from his room, a bag already slung on his shoulder.

"I'll be right back."

Dani hurried to pack the second Libby headed downstairs, doing her best to find what she needed without actually turning on the light or attacking her closet like a mad woman at midnight when she wasn't supposed to make any noise. She did, however, pack extra gloves.

Creeping silently out the door, she found Will already waiting and standing beside a triumphant Libby.

Next to her was a stone-faced Anders.

"Libby!" Dani hissed. "You promised."

"I didn't go and get him. He stopped me in the hall."

It was no use dropping the bags she was holding and pretending not to be sneaking away.

"We're going to Frovland." Dani chose her words carefully.

"And then to the Northern Forest, I imagine. I'm coming as well."

Dani frowned in confusion. "Why? Aren't you needed here?"

Anders barely blinked. "Something tells me I'll be needed there more,"

"Thank you." She really was grateful for the help … and doing anything without Anders felt wrong. Dani quickly caught them up on the night's events, which, to her surprise, didn't shock them as much as she expected.

"We should head out. Everyone is probably waiting for us already," Will reminded her once she'd finished.

"Right. Sorry."

Libby handed her a gem, but Dani waited until she and Will had blinked away first to leave. Anders would never let her go last, but she needed a second to breathe.

"I'm fine," she promised Anders when he narrowed his eyes ever so slightly at her.

"It's all right to not be. Libby explained the plan."

"I'll be fine," Dani amended, crushing the stone in her hand and letting her mind fill with images of Umbergrove. When she opened her eyes, she was there, a few feet from the group already waiting.

If her friends were shocked to see Ivy and then Anders, they didn't show it.

In fact, the only one who spoke was Everett, and he only uttered three words. "Time to go?"

Dani nodded, getting out her medallion as the group assumed formation around her.

Her third blink in under an hour.

It was simpler than the others and made Dani feel a lot less nervous, which she hadn't expected. Blitzspire always made her a bit nervous, but now, getting to Frovland was a relief.

"Anders and Libby are coming too?" Amery fell in step beside her the second they landed in Frovland's blue forest. Their siblings and friends walked ahead, clearly more comfortable on their second trip.

"Yep." Dani nodded, cupping her hand over her mouth to summon her whirlpool to let it take her into a secret underground base … as one does at midnight.

"Mystery, you are something else." Amery grinned when, in a sharp contrast to earlier, everyone jumped into the whirlpool with no fear at all.

Dani watched Libby disappear into the area below. "I'm going to consider that a compliment."

"Oh, it was one," he promised, stopping at the edge of the whirlpool and jumping.

Dani couldn't tell if he was being serious or teasing her, but she followed, landing in the holding room with perfect ease. Anders landed a few feet away.

"I don't have much experience with teenagers, but I didn't think they went out of their way to invite more adults along on missions that they themselves shouldn't be undertaking." Ivy was already waiting for them, leaning against the silver wall.

"We didn't have much of a choice," Dani admitted.

"Who is this?" Libby nodded toward Ivy as Anders took up a position in front of the kids.

"This is Ivy, our handler." Dani made the introductions since her friends clearly didn't want to.

"I'm in charge of the children and their safety whenever they do anything involving our organization," the older woman said.

"I guess that will be helpful," Libby conceded, not seeming to mind that Dani had forgotten to explain about Ivy.

Anders looked like he had seen a ghost.

"Ivy." His face was a mask of steel.

"Anders." Ivy inclined her head slightly.

Dani frowned. "You guys know each other?"

Ivy nodded but didn't elaborate. "I have everything Hugo wanted you to take, and Ember has already been alerted. She'll know when to come if she's needed."

Anders nodded. Dani had already explained her new dragon situation to him during her mission rundown.

"We have our stuff too." Amery held up the large satchel they had filled with food, supplies, maps, and gemstones.

"Good. We can leave, then." Ivy had already made it abundantly clear that she wasn't going to take orders from anyone else and held her hand out, walking over to the boys.

Everett obediently reached into the bag Amery held and grabbed a handful of the gemstones they had packed. Ivy took one for herself and handed another to Dani and then Libby. Amery and Everett passed the others out.

"Ready?" Will nudged Dani, who looked up from fussing with her gloves to see eight pairs of eyes on her.

"Sorry. Yes, I'm ready." After being so determined to do this quest and save her mom, Dani's nerves had finally kicked in, and the reality of what she was about to do weighed heavily on her shoulders.

Even before she made it to Breckindale, Dani had never been a stranger to the feeling. She'd been bullied her entire life and had her confidence smashed in the process, found out her entire life was a lie and learned she had a dangerous power in the same hour, and then barely had time to adjust to a completely new family before learning that she'd been born as the chosen one in an ancient prophecy. Even now, every single minute led her closer to the destiny that she still desperately wished she could run away from.

In a way, now she was. And despite the dangers, the fear, and the unknowns, Dani felt more ready than she ever had been to face a challenge.

Being a leader was not something Dani considered her strong suit, but somehow, it was supposed to make perfect sense. Now, she had an entire team she was leading and a mission that had been entirely her idea.

Dani just hoped she wouldn't blow it.

CHAPTER TWENTY-FOUR

According to Libby, blinking to the edge of the Northern Forest was the last easy part of this field trip. She had taken over as tour guide, dishing out most of the instructions since Anders and Ivy seemed to have a shared goal of staying as far away from each other as possible. Dani made a mental note to ask Anders why … mostly because Ivy scared her, but she hadn't gotten the chance yet.

Ivy was now leading the group, and Libby and Anders were flanking behind on either side as they approached the forest, staring at it as if it was the greatest enemy ever faced.

Dani wondered if, at least for now, it was.

"The second we step into the woods, there is no going back. Blinking isn't safe, and there are dangers around every corner. Make sure to stay alert, especially you six." Ivy leveled a sharp look at the kids standing in a clump and looking around at each other, confused.

"We understand," Will promised, interrupting whatever remark Amery had been about to make that surely would have ended horribly. Dani sincerely didn't want to be on Ivy's bad side.

"Good." With that, Ivy turned on her heel and marched into the trees.

Dani wished she had the confidence to do the same. Delacour had been just as bold, and she'd stopped a war.

"You need to stop comparing yourself to her." Will nudged her, not even trying to hide that he'd read her thoughts.

"I can't help it. I was born to be her carbon copy."

"You were born to be her heir," he corrected.

"Is there a difference?"

"You're not going to let a prophecy dictate your life."

Dani raised an eyebrow in response. That was all she'd been doing since being given the prophecy.

"Prophecies don't change. They can't be stopped."

"Until now."

Dani didn't quite have as much faith in herself as her brother did.

She frowned. "When did you become so determined to beat this thing?"

"Since you got it. But The Golden Eagle inspired me."

"Really?"

Will nodded. "Delacour wouldn't have created a whole organization and given you a dragon if she didn't intend for you to beat this. From what you explained earlier, your council genuinely cares and has to put time into this."

"They have," she conceded.

"Exactly. Delacour wanted to change things to make sure that you succeed. Comparing yourself is the absolute worst thing you can do."

Dani's smile was strained. "You should become a professional pep-talker."

"No, he shouldn't! Where is this enthusiasm when I'm panicking about potions?" Amery feigned indignation from behind Dani.

Dani smirked. "Usually trying not to panic about potions with you."

"I never get nervous about potions," Lydia bragged, never one to waste an opportunity to dog on her brother.

"That's because you actually study." Dani craned her neck to catch her best friend's eye. "Too much if you ask me."

Lydia liked to spend her entire lunch break poring over notes, claiming that since her session was in the afternoon, every spare minute counted. Dani hadn't argued with her the previous school year and hadn't even attempted to this year.

"And I get high grades, do I not?"

"Not as high as Eldridge," Amery remarked.

Lydia shrugged calmly. "He's in his own super genius category."

"Always has been." Everett pretended to be annoyed until his brother swatted him.

"Says the history buff," Eldridge shot back.

Everett went crimson. "Shut up!" he said, eyes glued to his shoes.

"There's no need to be embarrassed about it, Ev," Lydia encouraged. "It's a good thing, you know."

"Sure." He didn't look convinced.

"It is, promise." Dani had spent too much of her life being bullied for her knowledge to not make it her mission to ensure Everett was proud of his.

"Not to interrupt this moment, but I can't focus on keeping us safe if the six of you are going to keep bickering like this." Ivy didn't look back, but it was very clear that there was no warmth in her expression.

They all went silent.

Dani had expected at least a single argument from Amery or Lydia, but neither Varron made a peep of noise. Even Libby didn't offer a sarcastic comment to lighten the mood.

Ivy was already ruining the fun and they'd barely made a dent in the mission … or Dani assumed they hadn't. Ivy was now in charge of the map.

She would have preferred it to have been given to Anders, who at least would have shushed them more politely, but he seemed to not want to argue with her either.

"Okay. Now that you're all listening properly, we can go over my rules," This time, Ivy did turn around, pausing only so that she could fall in step with the rest of the group.

"Your rules?" Dani repeated, unsure if she'd misheard.

Ivy ignored the question completely, continuing on as if no one had spoken.

"Rule one: Trust has to be earned. I don't expect you to trust me already, and I certainly hope that you don't expect me to trust any of you yet either. Trust has to be earned, not given, and it's a waste to expect otherwise. Understood?"

Dani glanced around at her friends but nodded.

"Rule two: We're allies, not friends. I'm protecting you because it is my job. This isn't personal. The Golden Eagle wants me to ensure the safety of the Savior and her team, and that's what I will do, but I have no intentions of being your confidante or close friend. That's not my job or the job of any guard working with children."

Dani glanced over at Libby, expecting some kind of reaction, but Libby only met her eyes and shook her head once. When Dani turned to Anders, he was as stone-faced as ever.

"Rule three: Only address me if you have an urgent matter or are in danger."

And then she spun right back around and continued marching on as if she hadn't just made enemies out of a rather creative group of teenagers.

Dani couldn't read minds unless she took off her gloves, but she had a distinct feeling that her friends were all thinking the same thing, a rare phenomenon between the six of them. This consensus, however, was abundantly clear.

They were not a fan of their new handler.

CHAPTER TWENTYO-FIVE

Dani spent the next hour trying not to trip over things she couldn't see.

The forest was almost entirely pitch black, and although the lanterns they had brought helped, Dani was still wary of the roots and logs and other hazards that could and most likely would make her fall on her face. Her friends didn't dare make much of a conversation, especially when Ivy was in hearing range, so they followed in silence.

Dani decided to walk beside Anders instead, partly because she needed to breathe and partly because she could ask about how he knew Ivy.

Truth was, silence gave her mind opportunities to wage war, and dark forests and even less sleep offered a refreshingly bitter attitude. Right now, her mind was informing her of all the ways that she was failing to be a leader.

It was her job, her team, her organization, and she was doing absolutely nothing except blindly following a woman she'd never met when it was her mom that was dying.

Pathetic.

"I know that look," Anders told her after she'd tugged at her gloves for the umpteenth time.

"I'm just thinking," she promised.

"About?"

"Life."

"You're doubting yourself." Anders knew her too well.

There was no point in denying it. "Bingo."

"Why?"

"It's default at this point," she replied, glancing around at the dark trees on either side of their path, Knowing that danger could strike at any moment made the otherwise serene forest incredibly unnerving.

Anders cleared his throat, forcing her to turn back and face him. "It shouldn't be."

Dani paused before answering, averting her eyes to the path ahead. "I'm aware," she said finally.

"You are your own worst enemy."

"I know."

"So, stop."

"I've lost count of the amount of times you've said that exact line," Dani deflected, trying for a joke so she didn't have to launch into another explanation about her lack of self-esteem stemming from a difficult childhood and impossible expectations.

"Because you never seem to listen to it."

"I listen!" Most of the time, at least. Sometimes, Anders talked for so long that she ended up just tuning him out instead.

Anders raised one brow in question. "And then choose to ignore everything I say."

"You're thinking of Libby," Dani countered.

"Am I?"

She nodded insistently. "I listen to everything you say. I just don't always do what you suggest."

"Even when my suggestions are only to stop you thinking less of yourself?"

"I can't just stop my brain from doing its job," Dani argued.

"And I'm not saying that you have to; I'm just saying that judging yourself too harshly won't do any good now or in the long run. You give yourself far less credit than you should."

Dani shrugged the warning off, not least because she knew he was right. "Why do you bring that up so often?"

"Because someone has to."

"It isn't your job." Ivy's harsh words about the responsibility of bodyguards rang in her ears. Dani didn't exactly consider Anders a close friend, and she was aware that it was his job to stand by her, but he cared more about her well-being than a bodyguard who was only following orders would.

Anders only proved her point when he answered with, "My job is to protect you from all threats, including those you create in your own head. I will continue to do so until you start believing in yourself."

"I believe in myself." But the words felt hollow in her ears, a brittle lie.

And Anders called her on it without a second thought. "Do you?"

"Hey, guys." Libby cheerfully joined them, saving Dani from having to make up a lame excuse that would have been shut down just as swiftly.

"You've been awfully quiet," Anders told her.

"Well, I can't be loud in a pitch-black forest, now, can I?"

Dani had to admit that she had a point.

"So, what's up with you?" Libby settled her gaze on Dani.

"Nothing much."

"I don't believe that. Considering you were looking really deep in thought a minute ago, I want to assume that it's either power problems, stress, or the golden ticket with you: doubt."

Dani forced a smile on her face. "We have a winner!"

"Your sarcasm is improving." Libby snorted.

Anders coughed.

"What? I'm not placing blame, and neither should you."

"Do you need something?" Anders asked instead.

Libby absently began twisting her ponytail into a braid. "I'm here to help."

"I don't need a pep talk," Dani said. "I'm just a bit tired is all." She'd been awake for more than a day, and the lack of sleep was beginning to wear her down.

Her guard shrugged but didn't argue. "Then I won't give you one."

"Thank you."

"Sure." And then Libby returned to her spot on the other side of the main group.

Dani stayed.

"Stop. There's a clearing ahead," Ivy instructed.

"I think there's more than that." Amery pointed at something higher.

"What is that?" Lydia held her lantern high above her head, frowning in concentration at the dark sky.

Even with the lanterns, seeing anything farther than a few feet was difficult for any of them.

"A structure of some sort, it seems." Anders moved in front to get a better look, leaving Dani back with her friends, all trying to make out whatever it was that they had reached.

It took a few more minutes of walking, but eventually, the view became a lot clearer.

Ivy had been right about the mile-or-so-long stretch of grass. It was void of any trees or shrubs, but none of that was especially interesting. The interesting part was what lay in the center.

A giant skyscraper. Made out of gold.

CHAPTER TWENTY-SIX

Ivy may not have had much experience with teenagers, but she sure did enjoy telling them that they weren't allowed to do things. Despite the fact that she and Anders still hadn't said a single word to each other yet, they both refused to budge on the problem at hand.

Dani found it annoying.

"There's a tower that could potentially have what we need inside, and you're saying that we can't go in?" Dani didn't expect the Revere Root to be in the tower, but there could still be a chance that it was. If there was a chance, even a small one, then they should take it and investigate.

"Yes." Anders barely even paused to consider it before turning her idea down.

"Why?"

"We have no idea what could be in there, and if it is a trap, which the entire forest is filled with, then I'd rather not deal with that so early into this journey." Ivy sighed as if even the thought of such an inconvenience wounded her.

"But if one or all three of you go with us, then we'll be protected, right?" Eldridge made a good point, unfortunately one already anticipated by their handler.

"The risk may not be worth it. It is very possible that there is nothing in there, and the search would be pointless," Ivy argued, her tone filled with an air of finality.

Anders nodded his agreement. "Getting up there itself may prove to be a challenge as well. None of you have any experience with scaling anything, let alone a twenty-foot tower, and we took no proper climbing gear with us."

Dani could imagine herself climbing and then plummeting from such a great height far too easily. "Okay, but we could levitate up." The tower had a door, albeit a door that was impossible to enter through without a very, very tall ladder or possibly giant stilts.

"It could be locked," Ivy considered, following Dani's line of sight.

"But it could also just be closed," Will countered.

"And we could always break down the door if we had to." Amery's grin suggested that he'd already compiled a thorough list of different reckless possibilities to gain entrance.

Ivy's frown made it clear that she was not down to try any of them.

"He's not wrong." But no one was surprised when Everett jumped at the chance.

"I'm still against it." Ivy was the final word on anything that they'd get to do for The Golden Eagle, but Dani knew that Anders was the final word on her. Wearing down one would essentially wear down the other and at least allow someone to go up. Dani's only option was to do something that she didn't do often.

She argued. And argued. And argued.

And then her friends argued. And argued. And argued.

They all could be loud when they had to, and six kids talking over each other all at once had a terrifying and amazing effect on two already weary adults.

Anders tried to just close his eyes and pretend that everything was peaceful. It didn't work, and they didn't stop.

"Fine." Ivy gritted the word out. "A few of us can go up and take a quick look. Emphasis on quick. Understood?"

"Understood," Dani promised, glancing at her friends.

"Who is the strongest at levitation?" Libby asked, unsheathing her sword.

"Mystery," Amery answered with zero hesitation.

"Actually, it might be Will."

Dani was naturally gifted at most brytlyn skills, but her brother had a knack for levitation.

Ivy gave a sharp nod. "You can go up and see if the door is locked. I don't believe anything will attack from above, but come right back down once you're done."

"Yes, ma'am," Will said.

"Never fall." Ivy gave the tiniest hint of a smile.

Dani frowned. "Shouldn't you tell him not to fall?"

Ivy shook her head. "No, I shouldn't. 'Never fall' is what Golden Eagle operatives tell each other before or during missions. Delacour started it when she formed the organization, and we shortened the original version some time ago."

Dani and Will exchanged a look.

"Never fall if you can spare a jump … That's the original, isn't it?" Dani sucked in a sharp breath when Ivy nodded, eyes narrowed in surprise.

"Did Hugo tell you that?"

"I read it somewhere." Dani wasn't about to tell Ivy about the chest sitting in her dungeon. Not yet, anyway.

Ivy pursed her lips thoughtfully. "It must've been during Delacour's time or a few years later if the whole phrase was written. Hugo didn't want it being used in its entirety in case someone drew it back to Delacour."

"It looked really old," Dani conceded.

"The door is ancient!" Will called down, already levitating close to the tower. "And it's unlocked. I can open it."

"Should we all go or keep a few down here with Libby?" Ivy turned to Anders, looking uncertain for the first time since Dani had met her.

If Anders noticed, he didn't call her on it. "Down here isn't necessarily the safest option; otherwise, I would suggest splitting."

"I know." Ivy didn't sound surprised by his answer; if anything, she seemed to have been anticipating it.

"Will, stay up there!" Anders instructed, glancing up to make sure the prince was stable in the air before switching to face the kids on the ground.

"Five minutes, and then we come down. Is everyone comfortable levitating up?"

"As long as we don't have to hold it for over twenty minutes, I should be fine," Everett promised.

Ivy arched her brow. "You can hold your levitation for twenty minutes?"

"We all can," Lydia answered. "Everett is usually the first down, but the rest of us can at least go another five minutes."

"Dani can go a lot longer than that. Will too," Eldridge added, already getting into position.

For the briefest of moments, Ivy looked impressed.

"Libby, can you stay down and make sure no one is coming?" Anders masked it as a question, but Dani was guaranteed it was an order.

"Sure." Libby twirled her sword with astounding efficiency and gave a nod. "Have fun!"

"Anyone up for a race?" Will called down, somersaulting in the air.

"A race?" Ivy turned to Anders again when the five children formed a line. "What are they doing?"

"Something they really shouldn't when they can't see well."

Anders was too busy covering his eyes with his hand to watch the five of them rise together and then try to shove, pull, and trip each other trying to levitate up to Will, who was laughing hysterically as Amery almost hit a tree and Eldridge began flapping like a bird trying to maneuver around the others.

"No part of that was even remotely safe," Ivy quickly reprimanded, gliding smoothly up to their level with almost perfect grace.

"No, but it was fun." Amery dodged a pinch from Dani just in time.

Ivy shot him an ice-cold glare.

"He means that we will be on our very best behavior from now on," Dani translated as Anders joined them.

"Good," Ivy said, opening the small door and ducking inside. "No pushing, shoving, or whatever you five were doing back there."

For once, they listened and silently followed Ivy into the golden monstrosity.

"Well, this is … cheerful," Amery remarked dully.

The tower was larger than it looked from the outside but contained very little. Everything inside was solid gold except for a wooden crate and its contents.

"It's engraved." Lydia held up the bow from the crate, sleek wood with stars cut into the sides. The arrows and quiver slung over her shoulder had the same design.

"It's beautiful," Dani said, inspecting the bow.

"Do you want it?" Lydia offered.

Dani shook her head. "You can keep it. You'd probably use it more anyway."

"Can I?" Lydia turned to Ivy and Anders, who both stood near the entrance.

"It doesn't appear to be enchanted," Ivy conceded. "It would be glowing if it was. If you want, you can take it."

Anders nodded. "Libby has trained with a bow. She wouldn't mind giving you a few lessons if you'd like."

"Really?" Lydia practically glowed with excitement.

"If you stab me with that thing, I'm going to use the arrows as back scratchers," Amery warned.

"You're disgusting." Lydia scrunched her nose, turning to shield the arrows away from him.

Everett snorted. "You act like you wouldn't at least threaten him with them."

Lydia tossed her hair over her shoulder primly. "Of course I wouldn't. I have other ways of pestering Amery."

Ivy fixed them with a sharp look. "If you all are done here, we can head back down. Nothing else is in this tower, and I'd rather we kept moving."

A boom rocked the tower, showering them with a fine layer of dust.

"What was that?" Dani jumped back, heading for the door.

Anders expertly blocked her. "Stay here, all of you."

Ivy was already out of the tower and, by the looks of it, levitating down.

Dani heard swords clanging, never a good sign when only one brytlyn was supposed to be on the ground.

Anders blocked her view as he climbed out and then dropped,

levitating down safely, Dani hoped.

The six of them raced forward together, peeking out of the doorway and trying to get a good view from above, which proved far more difficult than anticipated. The darkness was still thick so early in the morning, and all that could really be seen were tiny ant-sized brytlyns. A handful wore cloaks; three others didn't.

A flash of gold was visible flying from above the trees.

"Is that…" Will didn't even finish the sentence before he got an answer.

"I think so," Dani said, exchanging a worried glance with her friends.

Suddenly, the puzzle pieces forced themselves together in Dani's head as she stared below at the situation on the ground.

She had to remind herself to breathe as they all silently watched the golden dragon circle the scene.

Ember was here.
And dragons only blinked if there was danger.

Dani twisted her fingers so tightly that the fabric of her gloves almost tore.

Ember was here, and Dani was pretty sure they were under attack.

CHAPTER TWENTY-SEVEN

"It's the Midnight Dragon." Dani almost couldn't bring herself to say the words. "They're here."

Will whipped around so fast that he almost knocked Lydia over. "What?"

"The people fighting down there are wearing cloaks. It has to be them." Dani couldn't think of anyone else who would want to interrupt the quest … or anyone who would venture to the forest willingly for that matter.

Lydia frowned. "How do they even know we're here?"

"I don't know."

Dani's heart sank all the way to her stomach.

Everett cleared his throat. "So, what do we do? They'll have our heads if we go down there to help."

"Well, the three of them are outnumbered, so I'd wager doing nothing isn't an option."

"We don't have weapons," Eldridge cautioned.

"I do!" Lydia held up her bow, forcing Everett and Dani to step back.

"But you don't know how to use it," Amery reminded her.

"What should we do?" Everett directed that question at Dani, like her opinion was the only one that mattered.

Dani anxiously tugged at her gloves. Anders had told them to stay put, and he would lose his mind if they disregarded a direct order. Then again, he couldn't freak out if he was taken down by the operatives who would do anything to get Dani out of the picture.

"I'm going down there," Dani decided. "You guys should stay here."

"What? Why?" Amery questioned, already prepared to jump into action.

"Because you'll be used as bait," Dani explained hurriedly. "If they get to you, then they'll have power over me."

"You should stay up here too," Will insisted.

"I'll be quick, promise." Dani flashed her most confident smile. "Ember!"

Ember flew to the door in barely two seconds, wings flapping elegantly in the night.

"I need to get down. Is it okay if I ride with you?"

Her dragon nodded, extending a wing. Dani figured that crawling onto a dragon's wing and then climbing onto its back was not exactly a safe maneuver, but she did it anyway.

"Please say that you have a plan for this, Mystery." Amery's expression was flooded with concern.

Dani took off her gloves and handed them to him, making sure her hands didn't make contact with his. "I have a plan."

Ember flew them down before Will could call her out on her lie. The second Dani saw what was transpiring below, she instantly wished that he had.

Ivy, Anders, and Libby were engaged in a battle against five Midnight Dragon operatives, each wearing a blue cloak with a flame. They had long swords made out of a darker metal that looked almost pitch black. Their wielders were skilled, but her team was winning, even with Anders and Ivy holding off two at a time … or they were until six more blinked there and one sword narrowly stabbed Anders in the side.

That was when Dani snapped.

Ember glided down and she jumped off, landing a few feet away from the fighting, allowing herself a second to make sense of what she was about to do. Dani knew the exact moment she was noticed because Anders spun to lead the operatives facing him away from her. Ivy was just as quick, meeting her eyes for the barest of seconds and shaking her head so subtly Dani almost didn't notice it.

Libby was facing away already, fully concentrated on her duel.

"Sorry, I don't remember inviting any extra help here," Dani called loudly, channeling all of Lydia's confidence as she feigned a yawn.

"Well, aren't you a snarky little thing," a man with hair the color of ash sneered, obviously delighted. "The Savior, I presume?"

"Dani." She tried to add in some of Amery's sarcasm. "I would say, 'Nice to meet you,' but it isn't, really."

"It is an honor to make your acquaintance, Dani." He held up a hand and his operatives paused, backing away from Dani's guards who, in turn, moved to defensive positions around her instead, all watching with curiosity and caution.

Dani rolled her eyes. "Never mind. Just call me Savior."

"Plucky girl, aren't you?"

She shrugged, crossing her arms. "I don't know about that … whatever your name is."

"Bartholomew."

"Bartholomew," Dani repeated, trying to keep the confusion out of her voice. "Okay. Well, I don't really appreciate you trying to kill my friends, so can you please leave and tell your leader that I say hello?"

Bartholomew didn't even pretend to consider the offer. "I'm afraid I can't do that, but the leader will appreciate the hello. She's a big fan."

"I bet she is … you know, until I kick her butt and ruin your plans and so on." Dani surprised even herself with the nonchalance. It masked the nerves she was fighting.

"And here I was told that you were quiet and polite."

"Usually, not with people I don't like."

"I was under the impression that we were bonding." Bartholomew adopted the most innocent of expressions, and Dani grimaced.

"Were we? I was under the impression that you were about to leave me alone."

"I can't do that, remember? My boss wants a chit chat with you in person."

"Maybe another time," Dani countered. "I'm a bit busy at the moment."

"Are you?"

"Yes, and I'm really not in the mood to talk." Especially not with a brytlyn intent on taking over her realm and forcing her family out.

"That's a shame."

Dani shrugged. "For you, I guess. I, for one, am perfectly fine with it."

Bartholomew tightened his jaw, his expression severe. "Okay. Here's how this is going to work: You are going to come with us, or the kiddos up in the tower will be given a dose of some of our newest poison supply and will die within the hour while there's nothing that you can do about it. Sound fun?"

"Not really." And with that lovely threat out in the open, Dani let the fear she'd been so vigilantly suppressing come to the surface, vivid red sparks dancing above her hands and illuminating her face in a bright red glow.

Bartholomew glanced at three operatives, and they took off toward the tower.

Dani let the emotions bloom inside her, stretching out her hands to create a spark sphere around her guards so that, at the very least, they would be safe. Dani had practiced it only once with Sir Hugo, but it had worked then, and she hoped with all her might that it would work now. The difficult part was holding it.

Dani easily launched a wave of sparks at the Midnight Dragons attempting to close in, knocking them back before she spun around to launch some at the operatives preparing to scale the tower.

"Ember?" she called, searching the sky.

The dragon shot through the trees like a bullet, landing dutifully beside her.

"I need you to go up and make sure that no one reaches the door."

Ember nodded and flew back up, leaving her owner alone once more.

Dani ignored the cramps in her stomach as she shot another tidal wave at the four operatives in front of her and then sent another behind her, wielding the sparks like a whip.

Her guards were still encased in the spark sphere, vigilantly attempting to fight through it. It may have been dwindling at the edges, but Dani was sure it could last another few minutes at the least. It would have to.

A sharp pain stung her gut, but Dani didn't stop the outpouring of power. Not when it was working so well. Everyone she wanted safe was safe, and the people she wanted gone kept getting pushed back, unable to overpower the sparks.

So, she kept going, losing track of how long the darkness became flicking spheres of ruby light around her. Dani could tell Bartholomew and his minions were getting tired and she was glad. She herself was growing exhausted and suddenly feeling very feverish.

Her hands were shaking and her legs felt numb, and for some reason, she couldn't seem to think straight and her throat was dry and breathing felt very hard.

Dani refused to stop. Her magic felt good. Strong. She had more sparks, and she was going to use them until she won.

One minute, the cloaked figures were trying to deflect sparks, and then they were gone, light still flashing from a blink.

Ember soared back down, making dragon noises that seemed to be celebratory.

Dani stopped her sparks, which were, at any rate, about to stop themselves, and then fell to the ground in an exhausted, sickly heap.

She saw three very blurry figures rush toward her, but her eyes didn't allow them to come into focus.

"Did we win?" Dani weakly wrapped her arms around her knees, hugging them tight as the cool grass touched her cheek.

Anders sat beside her. "We won."

Dani's head was spinning and black spots erupted in her vision, but she managed a smile. "Fantastic."

And then she blacked out.

CHAPTER TWENTY-EIGHT

Dani didn't know exactly how long she was unconscious, but she knew it was long enough for the darkness to become light that stung her corneas when she opened her eyes.

She must've swam in and out of consciousness half a dozen times because Dani had mangled memories of two people arguing. At first, she had thought it was her parents, but somehow, even with her brain turned to mush, she knew that it wasn't.

"… never should have come down."

"My job … not yours."

"This mission… It is."

The first few instances had been brief and the words sounded like gibberish, but as her body began to improve from its drained state, the conversation she was overhearing started to make sense.

"Dani would never let us fight for her."

"It's impossible to protect her if she doesn't let me do my job."

"Dani needs to trust you, and in order to trust you, she must like you."

"Well, I don't care if she likes me or not. I am simply doing my duty, as I've mentioned already and as you're well aware."

"Indeed."

The voices were familiar, but Dani couldn't place who they belonged to.

"Exactly why you should let me do my job, then, considering you can't seem to do yours properly."

"I have been protecting her for almost a year. Is that not my job?"

"Bodyguards are not supposed to bond with their charges. Is that not the first thing we learned in training?"

"At Elthorne, it was encouraged."

"Well, I obviously won't be bonding with any of them."

"I think you'll be surprised." Anders. That was Anders.

"I think y…" And that was Ivy, who trailed off the second she noticed Dani staring.

"What's going on?" Dani had opened her eyes just enough to see light peeking through the closed door.

"We're regrouping," Libby answered from beside it, gesturing to Dani's friends, asleep a few feet away. Then she jerked a thumb toward Anders and Ivy. "Those two have been arguing for hours."

"I remember." Dani grunted, forcing herself into a sitting position.

"How are you feeling?" Ivy asked the question like it was out of obligation. Dani didn't have to be a Sensor to see through it.

"Better. My head still hurts, though, and I feel like I drank salt water."

"That's what happens when you use too much magic," Anders told her.

"It stinks," Dani admitted. "Why are we back in the tower anyway?"

"Because you were unconscious, and staying out in the open wouldn't be an ideal circumstance safety-wise. Ember flew you up here, and we levitated in. Your friends were worried, but once we promised that you were okay, they calmed down," Ivy explained.

"We figured letting you all rest was a smart option for the time being," Anders added.

"How long was I out for?"

"Six hours," Libby said.

"We need to get moving, don't we? That's too long to have stayed here." Dani was already scrambling to her feet when Anders stopped her.

"Sir Hugo sent extra operatives to shadow us, and Ember has been circling the forest for hours. We're safe at the moment," he promised.

"How did they even know we were here?"

"That's what we've been trying to figure out," Ivy revealed quietly. "Hugo thinks we have a leak."

Dani paled. "He told me that I may know a traitor."

"The three of us took oaths, and we're all clear, if you were wondering," Libby offered.

"Who administered them?" Dani hadn't remembered hearing any other voices.

"Ivy did ours, and then Anders did hers. Hugo thought it might help you feel better about this."

"It does, I guess, but I didn't think you guys were traitors."

Anders gave a significant look toward Ivy. She didn't return it.

"We don't believe that it's a member of The Golden Eagle," Ivy stated, all business. "We are all watched incredibly closely by your council."

"Someone from Elthorne," Dani realized, immediately wishing that she hadn't. The thought consumed her entire brain in seconds.

"Possibly, but it could also not be," Anders warned her. "We don't know enough to place blame just yet."

Dani frowned. "The leader is a girl; we know that."

"And there are countless female brytlyns that could be leading that organization. That doesn't mean that she is necessarily someone that you know."

Ivy did have a point.

"For now, we should just focus on continuing on and getting the root safely and as fast as possible."

"Okay," Dani agreed, glad to be focusing on the real task at hand. "Good plan. Should I wake them up, then?"

"No need, Glove Girl." Amery offered a crooked smile as he stood, followed by Eldridge, Will, and finally Lydia, who was shaking Everett awake. "And here are the famous gloves, by the way." He handed them to her.

"Thank you." Dani quickly put them on. She hadn't had the time to panic over not wearing them, probably a good thing.

"You're welcome,"

Will practically strangled her with a hug. "That was stupid."

She hugged him back. "It worked, didn't it?"

"You could've gotten yourself killed."

"I know." Dani just wished her senses didn't still feel quite as dull. "But they already wanted to kill me before. Our birthday is coming up. I'm supposed to end it any day now."

"The prophecy still hasn't come true," Everett pointed out, rubbing sleep from his eyes.

"It will," Ivy affirmed. "But she'll win."

"That's good," Lydia said, seemingly trying to convince herself of the fact.

Ivy gave a curt nod. "For the time being, yes. Now, we should really leave."

"Everyone okay?" Dani asked her friends.

"Ready when you are, boss," Amery answered first, backed up by nods from the rest of the group.

"Good," Ivy approved.

Everyone but Dani levitated down, Lydia carrying her new weapon proudly. Ember met them on the ground, Dani on her back. Anders had refused to let her levitate, considering her condition, and the dragon had been more than happy to assist her grumpy owner.

Ember even insisted on carrying her all the way to their next stopping point: an underground tunnel.

"Anyone else think that this is seriously creepy?" Everett asked once Dani had joined them a few feet from the entrance.

"Me!" Lydia raised her hand high. "I didn't know that this forest has tunnels."

None of them had.

"It's definitely not brytlyn-made." Ivy stepped forward to inspect the edges.

"So, it's from the forest?" Will questioned.

"It appears so," Anders agreed.

Dani didn't understand it. Tunnels, especially ones as large as this one, couldn't have just formed naturally.

"Is that even possible?" Dani whispered to Eldridge.

"Magic." He shrugged.

In Breckindale, magic did work in weird and sometimes totally unconventional ways, but Dani still wasn't completely convinced. Still, she didn't argue when Ivy announced that they would have to go through it.

Turns out she wasn't the only reluctant one.

"Don't get me wrong, I love tunnels, but this one is kinda freaky," Will said, straying to the back of the group.

"Because it's made of dirt?" Dani asked, smiling when he grinned.

He shrugged. "Ours are way better."

"Agreed," Dani conceded.

"Agreed!" Amery called, peeking back out of the tunnel. "Now, come on! It's just like the east wing tunnel in Elthorne."

If only they knew how wrong he was.

CHAPTER TWENTY-NINE

"I hate mud." Lydia's complaint echoed through the tunnel like a ghostly recording. She took another step forward, cringing when her boot sunk into the sludge. "I really hate it."

Dani, who had mud seeping all the way to her socks, had to agree.

To Amery's credit, the tunnel did have similar dimensions to the one that ran through the east wing in Elthorne. Unfortunately, instead of weathered stone, this tunnel was made of roots, mud, and dirt that fell into everyone's hair and made breathing slightly difficult.

"At least it's not a swamp," Everett said, his ginger hair spotted with brown.

Amery coughed. "A swamp would smell better."

"That's not hard to imagine." Will swatted at the air in front of him.

"We're almost there," Dani promised, trying to ignore her mud-caked boots and debris-streaked hair.

"Are we sure that this is the best way to go?" Lydia asked, earning groans and sighs from every one of her friends.

A chorus of "Yes!" shouted back at her, each repetition more disheartening.

Lydia sighed. "All right. Just checking."

Dani didn't blame any of her friends for wishing for a way out, especially when the mud began to get thicker and she nearly lost her boot trying to walk further.

"Believe me, I never would have chosen this route if there was an alternative." Ivy grunted, sloshing through the muck miserably. "Unfortunately, there wasn't one."

"There needs to be," Lydia decided, taking a calming breath and another cautious step that produced a very unsatisfying squelch.

"Look on the bright side—we aren't presently being attacked." Eldridge, possibly the muddiest traveler, was also the only one who didn't seem to mind.

Lydia's eyes blazed with disgust. "Except by dirt. I hate dirt."

"You really are racking up enemies, aren't you, Lyds?" Amery teased, swiping at his brow and leaving a streak of mud behind.

She blew a strand of hair away from her eyes, frowning down at the muck below as if it had a personal vendetta against her. "Evidently."

"To be fair, this is kind of disgusting," Libby conceded, the first comment she'd made since entering the tunnel. Dani had expected her to be the first one to issue a complaint, but that honor had gone to Amery, beating out his sister by only a few seconds.

"No shower I take will be long enough."

"Oh, quit being so melodramatic," Amery told her, rolling his eyes. "It'll be over soon."

"This tunnel ends in less than a mile," Anders announced not long after. "I'm sure you can survive until then."

"Of course." Dani almost collapsed from relief. She almost collapsed, period, the mud rising and soaking her leggings up to her ankles.

Hearing that the end destination was coming up also seemed to spur on Lydia, who marched through as fast as she could, barely even flinching when her boots squished with every step and her purple leggings stained brown up to her knees.

"Are tunnels on earth usually underground in forests?" Amery whispered to Dani, sloshing forward to walk beside her.

"Not that I know of." Though, to be fair, she'd never paid much attention to tunnels, and her house hadn't been near any forests.

"Convenient."

Dani snorted. "Yeah, I guess so."

Amery coughed. "On the plus side, this will definitely make a good story when we get back. Think I could get extra credit in potions if I say that I was trying to collect ingredients?"

"I doubt it, mostly because mud isn't an ingredient in anything we've made this year."

"Why do you always have to be right, Mystery?"

Dani shrugged. "No clue. Why do you always have to be the insane one?"

Amery gasped. "Insane?"

"Sorry. I guess imaginative is a better word," Dani corrected, her boot getting caught in the mud. She wobbled unsteadily. "Mind giving me a hand? I think I'm stuck."

Dani reached a hand up, but she only swatted air.
When she looked up, Amery was gone.

She pried her boot loose herself, spinning around and splashing mud up to her knees. "Okay, very funny, Amery." Dani's annoyance became panic the second her brain processed what she was seeing. No one was behind her. The tunnel had gone silent, void of any sound that wasn't supplied by drips of dirt from above.

Dani dislodged her sinking boots again, nearly tripping over herself as she turned back around, half expecting her friends to have levitated ahead with her guards as a prank of some sort. They were known for that, weren't they?

But they hadn't. The cave was empty.

She was alone.

CHAPTER THIRTY

Dani didn't allow herself to panic until she'd made it out of the tunnel. At first, she decided to turn back, sloshing all the way in the other direction to check if her friends had somehow been left at the entrance by some weird magical circumstance, but all she was met with was mud and dirt.

She reached the halfway mark before finally turning back to make it out on the other side.
A two-mile walk through thick mud was far more difficult alone, but stopping meant getting stuck, and Dani couldn't afford to waste time. Her friends had all disappeared in the most dangerous place to go missing, and trying to figure out what had happened took up the rest of the time it took her to be free of the tunnel.

By the time she did, Dani's legs felt like jelly, and mud was clinging to her boots and leggings.
She allowed herself a few minutes to lay on the grassy field the tunnel let out to, silently hoping that the rest wouldn't cost her or her missing companions.

At the very least, they hadn't blinked, confirmed by the lack of gemstones and flashing lights that Dani was sure she would have noticed. As far as theories went, she had plenty, none of them plausible under the circumstances.

"Ember!" Dani had never been so grateful to see the golden dragon twirling through the sky. She picked herself up, waving her arms like a crazy person until Ember landed beside her. "I need you to look for my friends. They're somewhere in the forest." Or she hoped they were, anyway.

Ember nodded, extending a wing.

Dani shook her head. "I should keep going. The faster I get the Revere Root, the faster we can go home." If Anders was with her, he would've agreed, and she trusted his judgment more than even her own. Besides, the less time she had to spend in the Northern Forest, the better.

Ember soared back out of sight, leaving Dani completely alone for the first time since she'd arrived in Breckindale. She forced her mud-caked boots forward, focusing on the lack of shrubbery and trees around her instead of the possibility of being ambushed by the Midnight Dragon at any second.

She could take them by herself—she already had—but Dani wasn't sure how long her sparks could last. For the most part, her energy was improving, but her headache hadn't even come close to dissolving completely, and after the tunnel, Dani felt like taking another hour-long nap and waiting it out.

There was no path to follow, which made picking a direction slightly difficult, and after weighing her options, Dani just decided to start walking forward. To her dismay, there was a whole lot of nothing around her for at least another half hour, the sun beginning to peek through the clouds.

Another mile in, trees did begin to appear, much to Dani's relief, and with them came yellow flowers with tall stems and oval-shaped petals. When she went over to investigate, they were tiny butterfly-like critters with glowing wings swarmed around them. Flixies, Dani had learned, were rare creatures in Breckindale, and almost identical to the fireflies she used to catch in her backyard as a kid. When she'd brought that up to Amery, he'd explained that Flixies were an endangered species and, as such, couldn't be caught. They were, however, excellent trackers.

"Hello." Dani had never seen any up close, but she'd learned from school that to not scare them off, she was supposed to be quiet and polite. "I'm looking for the Revere Root."

The Flixies buzzed, assembling before her into two lines and leading the way to a stream so clear Dani could see every pebble under the pristine turquoise water. It was beautiful, but there were no plants in the area, kind of defeating the purpose. "I don't see anything over here." Dani felt a little silly talking to creatures that were smaller than her fingernails, but they were the only source of life around.

The Flixies buzzed, flying in a swarm around her. Dani barely had time to catch up before they flew off and around a jagged cliff, more out of place than the tower and tunnel combined. Then again, what stood behind it wasn't exactly ordinary either.

It was a hedge maze.

A hedge maze at least thirty feet high and twice as thick. Diverting around it meant swimming upstream in a harsh river, and the Flixies flew behind her, making the choice clear. "Thanks," Dani said, expecting the Flixies to follow her inside. They kept their positions guarding the entrance, so she just shrugged and went inside, not wanting to make them angry.

Dani knew that every maze had a trick to them, but puzzles had never been her strong suit.

She rammed into hedges with nearly every turn on her first try, and her strategy of taking only lefts and then only rights led to a similar result. Finally, Dani tried an alternate route, randomly picking left or right until it got her somewhere.

On her first left, she got a nasty scratch on her arm.

On her second right, she hit a dead end and almost gave herself another one hitting the hedge in frustration.

And on her third right-left combination, she found Eldridge Callisto laying against the corner.

CHAPTER THIRTY-ONE

"Eldridge?" Dani crouched down, releasing the breath she'd been holding when she saw his chest rise and fall. She poked him in the arm, only letting up when his eyelids fluttered. "Eldridge, wake up!"

"You can stop hitting me now." Eldridge pushed her hand away and sat up.

"Sorry. I got worried that something had happened to you." Dani apologized quickly, resisting the urge to hug him. She was grateful to see a familiar face more than she wanted to admit.

Eldridge rubbed his eyes, looking up in alarm when he took in their surroundings. "Other than being rudely awakened by an impatient princess, I'd say I'm fine. Are you?"

"I'm fine," Dani promised. "You're the one who disappeared."

He frowned. "Disappeared?"

Dani nodded. "From the tunnel. So did everyone else."

"You must've had a weird dream too." Eldridge lifted a brow, his gaze practically calling her crazy.

"A weird dream?"

Eldridge nodded. "In mine, we were fighting a giant mud monster. I think Libby ended up freezing it so we could escape."

Dani shook her head firmly. "This wasn't a dream, Eldridge. We were actually in a cave. Lydia complained for the entire time about the mud."

"Lydia hates anything that ruins her clothes." He snorted.

"Well, yeah," Dani couldn't argue with that, "but the tunnel was real."

"Positive you didn't have a nightmare?"

"Eldridge!"

"What? That's not uncommon for you."

Dani sighed. "Yes, but that's not the point. Do you remember how you got here?"

Eldridge grimaced. "Not really. I remember falling asleep in the tower. You were unconscious."

Dani didn't know how to explain to her friend that his memories had been wiped without freaking him out completely. Eldridge was logical, his brain dealing far better with facts than opinions. Despite the fact that Dani was trustworthy, he wasn't going to believe her without proof. Proof she unfortunately didn't have.

She still tried anyway. "I was, and then I woke up because Anders and Ivy were arguing. We traveled for a bit and then found a tunnel."

"Why would we go in a tunnel?" Eldridge wondered, brows furrowed in confusion.

Dani shrugged. "Because we had to. I'm not sure; we just followed Ivy."

"Where is Ivy anyway?"

"I don't know. I sent Ember to go and look for everyone. Like I said, you all disappeared."

"Did we blink?"

"No." Dani was sure of that, at least. "No, you didn't blink."

"The Northern Forest is supposed to have traps," Eldridge conceded finally, trying to convince himself of the fact.

"So, you do believe me?" Dani had expected more pushback and questioning.

Eldridge managed a smile. "I don't think you'd go out of your way to make something up."

"It happened," Dani said flatly.

"Okay, okay. Fine. I believe you."

Dani knew he didn't, but she appreciated the sentiment regardless. "We should go now."

"Go where? Why are we in a maze?"

"Flixies led me here when I asked them to lead me to the Revere Root. I'm not sure how you got here." Dani was just really glad that he was.

"Have you found it yet?" Eldridge asked, forcing himself to his feet.

Dani joined him, glancing around at the hedges surrounding them, fencing them in. "To be honest, I haven't really started looking. I've just been trying to escape."

"It's just a maze." Eldridge said the word like a maze was just an easily tackled school assignment.

Dani rolled her eyes, though she was glad to see him act normally. "Easy for you to say, Mr. Genius. Want to try to figure this out?"

"If you insist." Eldridge levitated halfway above the hedges before Dani followed suit, mentally kicking herself for not thinking of that shortcut first. The second he reached the top, an invisible force pushed him down, sending Eldridge spinning in midair.

"What was that?" Dani levitated back to avoid getting hit by a flailing limb.

"Forcefield of some sort." Eldridge rubbed his elbow where it had hit the edge. "The exit is three lefts and four rights from here. You got almost halfway."

"That's good," Dani conceded.

Eldridge's sigh had a whole lot of grumbling mixed in. "We have to walk."

Dani snickered. "You sound like Amery."

"He'd be a bit more whiny."

"A bit?" That was being generous.

Eldridge narrowed his eyes, considering. "Okay—a lot. Where is he anyway?"

"Like I said, I don't know."

"You don't know a lot about this, do you?" Eldridge was fighting a triumphant grin.

"Go figure," Dani retorted.

"How long was I out for?"

"An hour or so. To you, it must seem longer."

"It does," Eldridge said. "At least we've made some progress."

"That's a positive," Dani agreed, though it was outweighed by negatives at the moment.

Silently, they continued through the maze, taking one left, then two, and then finally a third that preceded two pairs of right turns, and then …

"Where's the exit?" Dani stared blankly at the solid hedge ahead of them, standing tall and gloating in their failure.

"It was here. I promise you it was."

"I believe you." Dani hadn't levitated as high, but she'd been able to see enough to be certain that an exit had, in fact, been where Eldridge had claimed it was. "This is another sick cosmic joke."

"If you mean it's a trap, then I'd be inclined to agree with you."

"We can't levitate." Dani had started pacing, searching the sky for any hint of gold. If Ember hadnt blinked to them, then, in theory, she wasn't in danger. On the other hand, Emer could be busy saving everyone else from an equally dangerous task to come to her aid.

"Blinking isn't safe," Eldridge reasoned, his brows furrowed in concentration as he stared at the hedge.

"We're stuck." Dani sighed, reality setting in and making her want to punch another hedge.

They were trapped.

CHAPTER THIRTY-TWO

"Remind me again how this is helping?" Eldridge asked, sitting with his back to a hedge.

"I'm getting us out!" Dani called down, grabbing at the twisted roots of the hedge opposite his, pulling herself up. They couldn't levitate away, but she could climb up and over, which was her plan.

"You haven't even gotten five feet up yet."

"Thank you for that lovely piece of encouragement."

Eldridge cleared his throat. "I'm just trying to make sure you don't break your neck when we can't get you to Cornelius."

"I'll be fine." Dani grunted, wishing that she wasn't quite so far from the top when her foot caught.

"I'd believe that a lot more if you almost didn't fall three seconds ago."

"You could help, you know. Figure out a better plan to get us out of here." Especially since Dani's plan wasn't going as well as she'd hoped.

"I am. Safely. From down here." Eldridge smirked.

"Well, I, for one, am going to find a solution."

Eldridge rolled his eyes. "And I won't?"

"Not by sitting all the way down there." Dani found another foothold, grasping at a higher root.

"And you're making so much progress from up there."

"I am." Though it would have sounded a lot more convincing if she wasn't so short of breath.

Or dangling off a hedge.

Dani climbed higher. "If we had a sword, we could just cut through it, assuming magical hedges work the same as normal ones."

"I don't think anything works normally here," Eldridge countered.

Dani stared up. She still had more than half of the foreboding plant wall to go. "That might be the point."

"It's why no brytlyns ever come here," Everett said. "The entire forest is traps on traps on traps."

"So we have to be smarter." Dani wished her solution didn't sound quite as impossible.

"Smarter than a forest?"

"Smarter than a *magical* forest," Dani corrected.

"Big difference," Eldridge retorted.

"I'm choosing to ignore that. Now, how do we outsmart magic?"

Eldridge paused only for a second. "By using magic."

"Actually," Dani was prepared to argue, but ... "That's not a bad idea."

"I have good ones from time to time," Eldridge deadpanned, standing up and holding his hand out, a ball of light flickering above his palm. Dani jumped down from the hedge right before he shot it.

The hedge lost a few layers but was still very much intact, not the result they'd been hoping for.

"Together?" Dani checked, already pulling one of her gloves off.

"Sure."

The hedge was met by Eldridge's sphere of light, followed almost immediately by Dani's sparks. It didn't burst into flames like they were aiming for, but a hole at least big enough to crawl through was created. They wasted no time in using it.

"Um, hello." Standing just outside the exit was a creature that Dani didn't recognize from any school textbooks she'd read, or any book in Elthorne's library for that matter. Two feet tall, with green skin the texture of tree bark, the creature wore a dress of flower petals woven with roots and vines. Her hair was made of moss and reached her shoulders in tangled curls. She looked childlike, with large, glassy eyes and thick lashes.

"Hello," Dani replied politely, glancing at Eldridge quickly. He only shook his head.

"I'm Daisy." The creature curtsied with surprising grace.

"I'm Dani, and this is Eldridge."

"You're a princess." Daisy smiled, showcasing two rows of stocky green teeth.

"I am," Dani answered.

Daisy frowned at Eldridge. "You're not a prince."

Eldridge snorted. "Definitely not."

"He's a lord, technically," Dani corrected, earning an elbow to the side.

Daisy didn't seem to notice. "Come on, we have to hurry if we don't want to be late."

"Where are we going?" Dani wanted to know.

Daisy only smiled again. "To visit my queen."

"Your queen?"

"Queen Noralee of the Aurelias is expecting us."

"Aurelias?" Eldridge repeated the word as if he'd never heard it before.

"The forest folk," Daisy explained, marching forward and leading them away from the maze. Dani and Eldridge followed.

Despite being two feet tall, Daisy was fast, springing through the forest in a flurry of leaps and turns. They didn't have to go far, stopping in a mossy cave that fortunately contained no mud. Daisy led them inside, walking to the center of what appeared to be a moss rug.

"This is the entrance to Sylvaine, the home of us Aurelias. Brytlyns don't often travel here, but my queen wants an audience. You must be respectful and never raise your voice."

"We got it," Eldridge assured her. "How do you get to Sylvaine?"

"You jump—well, I suppose fall is a better word."

"Jump?" Dani tried to keep the skepticism out of her voice.

"You have to jump. That's the only way it works."

For someone who jumps into a whirlpool daily, this should be easy," Eldridge reminded her before jumping easily, getting swallowed up by grass before his feet even landed back down.

"It doesn't hurt," Daisy promised. "You'll barely feel it."

Dani sighed. "I hope so." And then she jumped into the ground.

CHAPTER THIRTY-THREE

"What do you think?" Daisy's pride lit up her whole face as she twirled around.

"It's amazing," Dani breathed, barely able to comprehend her surroundings.

"I imagine that for brytlyns, it does look extraordinary."

That was an understatement. Sylvaine was almost a realm in itself, with an entire fortress, lake, and village inside the underground sanctuary.

Daisy served as tour guide, leading Dani and Eldridge up a winding road that led to a castle almost as large as Elthorne but better resembling the tall spires of Crystalium. Flowers covered the stone walls in varying shapes and hues of blue and purple, which, according to Daisy, were Queen Noralee's favorite colors.

Eldridge found it odd that a species with such a small stature needed high buildings, and Daisy patiently explained that the castle had been there long before her species, and when the Aurelias had inhabited it, they'd voted against making any changes.

Dani was more impressed with the architecture than the history. The interior was just as stunning as the outer walls. Strands of flowers hung from the ceiling, and the foyer had shards of crystals that hung so low both Dani and Eldridge had to duck on the way to the throne room.

"Are these all of the Aurelias who live here?" Dani asked when two guards in moss green armor opened the double doors their guide had led them to.

"Just the Queen's court and the nobility," Daisy answered.

"Huh." Dani's parents had never invited the nobility to watch official proceedings or meetings with their high council, and she'd expected that other monarchs did the same in their realms.

"Dani, look." Eldridge pointed to the side of the aisle where many regal and very tiny Aurelias stood beside Lydia and Everett, both looking confused but relatively unharmed.

They rushed over before a guard could stop them.

Dani made it first. "Are you guys okay? What happened?"

"We're fine," Everett promised. "And as for your second question, we aren't really sure."

Lydia nodded her agreement. "The two of us and Amery woke up in a cave, and then we fell into this place, and the Queen made us her special guests."

"What's the last thing you guys remember?" Eldridge asked.

"The tunnel,. Everett answered without a second thought. "We were all together, and then we disappeared, and everything went black."

"So, you guys do remember the cave. I'm so glad." Dani blew out a sigh of relief.

"Does everyone else not?" Lydia glanced at Eldridge and Dani, thoroughly confused.

"Eldridge doesn't; his memory was wiped. He only remembers falling asleep in the tower."

Eldridge crossed his arms. "So, the cave really did happen?"

"Yes!" Dani replied impatiently.

"Okay, okay. I said I believe you." He held his hands up in surrender.

Lydia frowned, staring at the empty space behind her friends. "Where's Will and the guards?"

"We don't know," Dani admitted. "I haven't found them yet."

"Maybe they're with Amery. He was escorted away a while ago. We think he could be in the dungeon."

Dani's eyes widened in alarm. "The dungeon?"

"It's just a theory. He could be anywhere."

"Did you guys even know that an entire species existed here?"

Everett shook his head. "No, it gave us a pretty nasty shock when we got here. Lydia screamed."

"I did not!"

Daisy waddled over and tapped Dani on the arm before Everett could argue. "Pardon me, but the Queen is expecting you, and she dislikes waiting."

"Of course."

Everett frowned, his whole head bowed to see the small creature. "Who's this?"

"Daisy. She found us," Everett explained.

"Nice to meet you all." Daisy curtsied.

"Hello," Lydia said, nothing if not an effortless social butterfly.

"Want to come?" Dani nudged Eldridge.

"I'll stay here and watch. Have fun."

Dani gave a pained smile, which Daisy seemed to notice in two seconds flat. "Don't worry. Her Majesty is quite kind and generous."

That at least was a relief … or it was until Dani actually had to face the Queen, sitting regally on a throne that barely reached Dani's shoulder. Despite Dani practically being a giant in comparison, Queen Noralee held herself in a way that demanded respect.

Daisy dipped a curtsy, and Dani quickly followed suit, grateful that her many etiquette sessions on the subject were paying off. "Your Majesty, this is Princess Dani."

"So, you must be the brytlyn that has been exploring my forest." Queen Noralee's voice was more high-pitched than Dani had expected, and with a better view, she looked a lot younger as well.

"We didn't know it was your forest," Dani apologized.

"No, I imagine that you didn't. Though it is always nice to see fellow royalty." Queen Noralee's voice was childlike and sweet, even when serious. "Your Amandine's daughter, aren't you?"

"Yes," Dani answered, confusion seeping into her answer.

Noralee crossed her arms over her elaborate purple gown. "You look just like her."

"You've met my mom?"

The Queen nodded. "Only once when I was Crown Princess. She was very kind to me."

"Thank you." Dani wasn't surprised to hear that. Amandine was kind to just about everyone.

"How is she doing? Please do tell her that I'd love to catch up soon now that I am ruler."

Dani braced herself before giving her response.
"She's dying."

Noralee put a pudgy green hand to her heart. "My deepest sympathies." She looked around at her court, all of whom were silent. "Ahem!"

"Our deepest sympathies on your loss. We wish you peace and prosperity," They said monotonously.

Dani looked around uneasily. "Thank you."

Noralee cleared her throat, back to business. "I have heard from some of my scouts that you've been looking for the Revere Root. Is that true?"

Dani nodded. "We need it to help my mom."

The Queen's concern melted into an excited smile. "Just have ours!"

"Really?"

"We harvest it here. Believe me, we have plenty to spare."

Dani really hadn't been expecting that.

"But first, I would need to check with the future king."

"Future king?" Only one throne sat on the dais, and it was already taken.

"Yes." Noralee giggled, her green cheeks blushing pink. "Guards, bring out his throne!"

Six of the guards flanking the queen marched behind the blue curtain behind her, returning back with a navy blue throne.

And on it was a very grumpy Amery Varron.

"This is your future king?" Dani wasn't sure whether to be concerned or amused. "He's thirteen."

"And I am only fourteen. Not that much difference."

"You're queen at fourteen years old?"

"My father put me in charge last year when he resigned. I'm incredibly mature for my age. Do you see any of my delightful subjects objecting?"

Dani turned to glance at the nobles, all of whom stayed silent. "No, I do not."

Noralee folded her hands primly on her lap. "Exactly. I'm doing a splendid job."

Dani offered a polite smile. "Of course, Your Majesty. Unfortunately, Amery cant stay and rule with you; he has to return with me and my friends."

"You know him?" Noralee fixed her gaze first on Amery, and then on Dani.

"He's my friend. And three of my other friends are over there." She pointed down the aisle.

"Yes, yes. My new guests." Noralee waved at them.

"May I speak, Your Majesty?" Amery had been silent until that point, growing grumpily on his tiny new chair.

"Of course, Blondie."

Dani almost laughed at the nickname, but Amery's expression killed her jokes.

"Mystery is right, and I really don't want to be your king either. No offense. You seem like a great person, but I just don't think I'm qualified for this."

"Of course you are, Blondie; don't worry about that." Queen Noralee waved off the concern with a well manicured hand.

"Okay, but Amery can't stay here. He's not an Aurelia," Dani pointed out.

"Oh, yes, I know. It's perfect! My subjects deserve the best ruler possible, and he's absolutely hilarious."

Dani narrowed her eyes. "Amery Varron is the best ruler possible?"

Noralee frowned. "Who?"

"Blondie."

"Oh, no. I was talking about me. I'm a great ruler, and he's funny."

"He doesn't want the job." Dani wasn't sure how the Queen wasn't understanding, but she tried to keep the frustration out of her tone.

Being sent to the dungeon was not on the Epic Forest Bucket List Dani had made in her head.

"Because he's so nervous about ruining my perfect little kingdom. That's so kind of him."

"He can't live here. He already has a house."

"But my palace is more than adequate. I've already given him his own suite, and his sister and redhead friend each have their own too."

"This is kidnapping!" Dani exclaimed.

Noralee gasped. "I'm not kidnapping anyone! The blonde and ginger brytlyns can leave whenever they want. When Blondette and Ginger Number One arrived here, they were unconscious and severely dehydrated, which I helped with out of the goodness of my heart."

"Thank you for that," Amery cut in, hunched over in the throne and looking supremely uncomfortable.

"Well, I didn't want them to die! Brytlyns have always been kind to me, and they deserve the same in return." Despite her dramatics, Queen Noralee did seem to have a good heart … even if it did have a crush on Amery.

"But you're keeping a brytlyn here as your consort."

"And he is perfectly happy here." Noralee clapped her hands. "Now, I have tea in an hour and subjects to attend to. Your friends can all stay and wait for us to get the root and gifts for you. Daisy will escort you out, and you can wait in the cave, Princess."

"Why?" Dani hadn't even been rude to the Queen. A little short, yes, but definitely not impertinent enough to deserve to be put in the Aurelia version of a time-out.

Noralee adjusted her flower crown impatiently. "You are threatening my future king."

"I'm not threatening him; I'm just being honest about the fact that you taking my friend is wrong."

"I'm not taking anything. He is not property."

Dani almost snorted. "I'm glad you realize that."

"Excuse me?"

"Your Majesty, a word," Amery interrupted, charm intact and ready to rush to Dani's defense.

"Excuse me." Noralee smiled and shifted in her throne, completely turning her back on Dani, who instead met Eldridge's eyes from all the way down the aisle and rolled her eyes.

Amery and the Queen only spoke for a few seconds, but Noralee sighed very loudly and turned back to the princess standing in front of her.

"You may stay a few hours here as well, only because my darling future king requests it. And then you will get your stuff and save Amandine."

"Thank you," Dani said, curtsying again, albeit less respectfully.

And so she let the Aurelia guards lead her away from the throne room, wondering just how she'd ended up making an enemy out of a forest queen.

CHAPTER THIRTY-FOUR

"I hate this place." Dani paced her trillionth lap, stomping on the moss rug. She'd been given the room closest to the guard tower by Queen Noralee's request, and except for the bed, the flowers hanging near the door, and the rug under her feet, everything else was stone.

"You and me both," Eldridge agreed.

"My brother is engaged to an Aurelia. How do you think I feel?" Lydia grumbled.

"Awful?" Everett guessed, laying on the bed and staring at the ceiling. "'Cause that's how I feel now that half of our group is missing."

"Ember is looking," Dani promised. "They're somewhere in the forest, and she has the best view."

"At least you didn't lose your memory." Eldridge snorted.

"How does that even happen?" Dani wondered aloud, pausing for only a second before continuing her pacing.

Lydia propped her chin in her hand. "Considering the way that we disappeared from the cave, I think it's safe to say that magic works differently here."

Eldridge coughed. "That's what I said."

Dani frowned. "But it's still Breckindale. Why would magic be weird in a forest only?"

"Because it's the most dangerous place in the realm," Everett guessed.

"Every realm has different rules," Lydia maintained. "That's not a new concept."

"But it's the exact same realm!"

"No one can fully understand how magic works, Dani. You, out of all of us, should know that."

"I know it, I just don't love it," Dani grumbled, spinning on her heel to complete another lap. "Everything here is a trap, and it's really getting on my nerves."

The boys murmured their agreement.

Lydia jumped up. "Okay, new problem: How are we getting Amery out of here?"

"Maybe we can try to reason with the Queen?" Eldridge suggested, earning dubious looks from Lydia and Everett.

"Fat chance." Dani snorted.

Eldridge ignored them. "If we can make her understand that Amery doesn't want to be her king and that he logistically can't, then maybe she'll let him go."

"Key word is maybe," Everett said. "She does seem kind of attached."

"It's awful," Lydia complained.

"Agreed," Dani said.

Everett shrugged. "If all else fails, Amery could use his speed and escape. Aurelias don't have powers like we do."

Dani stopped pacing. "They don't?"

"No, the ones Everett and I talked to said they didn't have magic. At least, not the kind that we have. They are expert forgers and gardeners, though," Lydia explained.

"That's good news for us," Dani muttered, more to motivate herself than her friends. "We get the root and can go home."

A sharp knock on the door made them all jump.

Dani reluctantly opened it, resisting the urge to slam it closed when a handful of miniature guards stared up at her.

"The Queen is requesting the presence of you and your party in the throne room," a guard who Dani hadn't seen earlier said.

"We'll be right there," she promised, glancing back at her friends who had assembled behind her. To them she said, "Logic first, then speed."

"Got it," Lydia confirmed, and they started their walk to the throne room, which was only a few hallways away.

They entered through the side doors closest to the Queen's throne, though Noralee was standing when they entered. Amery was beside her, noticeably less grumpy when he saw his friends, rushing to stand beside his sister the second they entered.

Noralee sighed. "Blondie is free to go with your group."

Dani had to stop her jaw from dropping. "Seriously?"

The Queen nodded. "I have now realized that he doesn't want the job because of reasons that do not involve ruining my kingdom or hurting my people. He doesn't belong here, and I don't want anyone here who doesn't want to be."

"That's very nice of you," Dani said carefully.

"I'd like to think so." Noralee waved over one of her guards who gave Dani a potted plant. "Here is the root you requested."

"Thank you." Dani handed it to Lydia. "I'll tell my mom you said hi, though I'm sure she'd want to come in person as soon as she's able."

"I look forward to it. Now, I have one more gift that I must give to you."

Dani raised an eyebrow, warning signs flashing in her brain. She hadn't asked for anything else.

"Marmaduke!" Noralee's shrill voice made everyone's ears ring as she summoned an Aurelia with a bright purple tunic and feathered hat. "Bring the gift."

"It's right here, Your Majesty." Marmaduke placed a long, thin box in the Queen's hands, and she carefully opened it.

Dani tried to get a peek inside, just in case it was a poison or weapon of some sort, but Marmaduke blocked her, despite being shorter than both the Queen and guards.

The Queen smiled and gleefully gave a twirl. "For you." And she handed it over to Dani, who frowned, her prediction correct.

"What is this?" Dani examined the sword. It had crystal instead of metal, and the hilt was leather.

"When my great grandmother was ruler, she formed a friendship with a brytlyn named Delacour. I trust you know of her?"

Dani nodded, twisting her gloved fingers together.

"After the royal family was overthrown, the rebels at the time threatened our people. It was a very dark time. Delacour saved us, and as a result, we offered her this sword we'd forged."

"It's stunning," Dani breathed, truly meaning it.

"That it is." Noralee continued, "She kept it until a few weeks before her passing, returning it back to my great grandmother and asking that the sword be kept safe until it could be given to her heir. That's you, isn't it?"

"It is," Dani admitted.

Noralee smiled, proud of her guess. "Well, then, Longlive now belongs to you. Use it well."

Dani glanced down at the hilt, adorned with intricate patterns. "Longlive?"

"That's the name our forgers gave it. It's a worthy title for a sword belonging to two worthy individuals."

"Thank you."

The Queen brightened. "Aurelias have always lived harmoniously in Breckindale, and I hope that we can continue to do so while you fight and win your battle."

"Of course."

"Good. You're all free to go now."

Guards escorted the group back down the aisle, two others handing Lydia her bow and quiver and then the boys their satchels. Daisy met them at the doors and led them all the way out to where they'd entered the underground mini-realm earlier.

"This will take you back to where we came through," Daisy explained.

"How do we get back up to the cave?" Dani asked.

"Step on the platform," Daisy explained. "You'll be up in a second."

"This sounds fun." Lydia stood beside Dani with the boys right behind.

"Maybe it's like an elevator," Dani offered, staring up at the hole in the moss above them.

Eldridge tapped her on the shoulder. "An elevator?"

"Human contraption," she clarified.

"Is it scary?" Everett spoke up.

Dani shook her head firmly. "Not at all."

"I'll take your word for it." Lydia barely could get the sentence out before they were catapulted up, landing with a sharp jerk in the cave.

"Anyone else feel queasy?" Amery asked, clutching his stomach.

Both Callisto twins raised their hands. They did look a little green.

Lydia fiddled with her bow impatiently. "As much as I'd love to stay here and let you three puke in here, can we please get out of this cave?"

"Gladly," Amery agreed, leading the way out, walking faster with his speed.

"Well, you five certainly have had fun." The voice was cold, alert, and sharp.

Dani grinned. "Hey, Ivy."

Their handler offered the ghost of a smile. "Hey, yourself. We've been worried sick."

"We?" Dani questioned.

"Yep." Will followed behind, with Anders beside him.

"You okay?" Anders asked Dani carefully, staring at the sword in her hand.

"I'm good," she promised.

"This is great!" Amery cheered, still ecstatic over getting out of Sylvaine. "The team's back together."

CHAPTER THIRTY-FIVE

Dani was so relieved to be leaving the Northern Forest that she didn't care how exhausted and dirty she was.

She didn't even care that the main topic of conversation was her sword—or, more specifically, its name.

"I like Longlive. It fits," Will approved.

Everett frowned. "Because we want her to live long?"

"Because it's clearly an awesome sword name for a Savior," Amery countered.

Eldridge slung his backpack over his shoulder. "Yes, because that should always be the first priority for Dani."

"Yes," Lydia maintained. "It should."

Dani examined the crystal weapon now in her care. "I don't think I'm going to change the name. But I probably should learn how to use it."

"I can train you."

Dani hadn't expected Ivy to offer.
She also hadn't expected Anders to agree to the offer on her behalf.

She hung back to walk beside him as they continued on, sword in hand. Ivy was seven steps ahead, as expected, and Lydia was playfully bickering with the boys quietly while Libby kept them in check.

Dani and Anders hung back a few steps.

"Why do you want Ivy to teach me if you're my bodyguard?" She'd expected him to insist on teaching her, using his title and position to get priority in the matter.

"Ivy is the best swordsman I've ever met. You deserve the best possible training, and if it's with a sword, then it would be with her."

Dani's eyes narrowed. "You really trust her, don't you?"

"I've known her a long time," Anders noted.

"I knew it!" Dani beamed. "Did you two used to train together at the academy?"

"We did," Anders conceded.

"Why do you guys hate each other, then? Were you enemies or something way back when?"

"Something like that, at least at the beginning. Eventually, we became best friends." The corners of Anders's eyes crinkled at the memory.

"Huh. I can't picture that."

Anders knit his brows. "Why not?"

"Well, you aren't really friends with any of the guards at Elthorne."

"Because we are coworkers."

"But you're with them every day," Dani retorted.

Amery sighed. "Usually giving orders."

"I can't imagine you at Libby's age either."

"Are you calling me old?"

Dani didn't even try to deny it. "Well, you are,"

"I am not!"

"And how long ago exactly was your tenure at the academy?"

Anders crossed his arms. "I'm not answering that."

Dani did the same, albeit with a lot more difficulty. "And you didn't answer my question earlier. Why are you and Ivy so cold to each other now? I feel like if I suddenly got to do something with one of my friends in thirty or forty years, I would love it."

"I don't feel comfortable divulging this information to a teenager." Anders was a pro at sidestepping questions he didn't want to answer, especially if Dani was the one asking.

"So, there is more to the story than that. Noted." Dani grinned. "Did you guys date or something? Compete for a job? Work together?"

Anders said nothing, staring straight ahead.

Dani's smile tightened. "Okay … What non-expression is this?"

Anders took a deep, calming breath before answering. "Dani, this is not a conversation that we need to be having right now."

"I just want to know why you want me to trust her so badly if you barely look at her."

"Because I was married to her," Anders said finally.

Dani screwed up her face. "I didn't know you were married."

Anders kept his expression blank. "And now you do."

"Huh."

"As much as you know I enjoy our conversations, why don't you go talk to your brother? He's been anxious to see you."

"Okay." Dani got the impression that Anders just didn't want her to press anymore, so she dutifully walked over to her brother, who was clutching the Revere Root to his chest like it was his most prized possession.

Will was so excited that they could go and save Amandine that he didn't stop rapid-fire chatting the entire way to the edge. Ivy turned back as if to shush him a few times but apparently thought better of it and let him have the victory, quickly shared by the boys who never ignored a chance to celebrate something.

Dani instead decided to walk with Ivy, who she had to thank anyway.

"Danielle." Ivy slightly inclined her head.

"Ivy." Dani didn't know how else to respond.

"Do you need something?"

Dani nodded. "Thank you for offering to train me. I really appreciate it."

"Swords are useful weapons only if you know how to wield them.

Yours can be very powerful with the proper technique."

"Anders said that you're the best swordsman he knows," Dani said.

"He's a very close second," Ivy revealed. "We were top of our class."

"He mentioned that you guys went to school together." Dani picked her explanation very carefully.

"I heard."

"We were all the way back there."

Ivy actually smiled. "I have sharp senses … and already gave him permission to tell you the whole story. He said that you'd ask."

Dani frowned. "When?"

"You were unconscious," Ivy explained. "And he said that it would help you trust me if you knew."

"He's not wrong," Dani conceded.

"But he's not completely right either," Ivy filled in.

Dani tugged at her gloves. "Lately, I haven't known who to trust."

"And that's fair. I don't hold it against you." Ivy stopped at a clearing. Turning around to face the group, she said, "We're here."

Amery objected, looking around. "This isn't where we entered."

"Different side, still an exit." Clearly, Anders didn't want an argument.

No one challenged him.

The second they stepped out of the forest, the sky darkened into a vivid sunset.

"It's already dusk," Lydia observed.

Dani frowned. "How is that possible?"

"I don't know," Libby admitted, three words that she did not say often.

"We should head back," Anders ordered.

Ivy nodded her agreement. "I have to return to Blitzspire, but I'm sure that you'll all be requested for a meeting later."

"Here. I don't think my dad will react well if he sees this." Dani handed Longlive to Ivy, and Lydia followed suit, handing over her bow and quiver.

"I'll keep them safe," Ivy promised, double-checking that Anders was holding the Revere Root before crushing the gemstone she'd procured from somewhere. Then she was gone.

Everett pulled a handful of gems out of his bag and started handing them out. "Should we all head to Elthorne, or are you guys okay with going alone?"

"We should probably go alone," Will decided. "I doubt any of our parents will be happier if we stick together."

"Agreed," Lydia said.

"Here's hoping we aren't grounded for life." Everett grimaced.

"Never fall," Amery said, startling everyone. "What? Isn't that what we're supposed to tell each other now?"

"Going home isn't a dangerous mission," Will said.

Amery shuddered. "It is when your parents have already threatened extra study time."

Dani couldn't help but giggle. "Your parents threatened you with studying?"

Lydia grinned. "Oh, yeah. It was awesome."

"I'm so glad you enjoyed my suffering." Amery gave a sarcastic smile.

"I always enjoy your suffering," Lydia said cheerfully, smashing her gem. "Bye, everyone!"

"Team. Mystery." Amery acknowledged the Callistos and Stallards, gave a mock salute, and then blinked away.

"Keep us updated about your mom, okay?" Eldridge was a lot more serious, as he tended to be.

"Of course," she promised.

And then the Callistos were gone, leaving the royal twins and two guards at the edge of a forest.

They didn't stay long.

When Dani, Will, Anders, and Libby arrived at Elthorne, everything dissolved into complete chaos. Guards were everywhere, crowding them, separating them, shepherding Dani and Will up the stairs and straight to their parents' suite, where nothing seemed to have changed at all. The Magicals stood in the hall, Cornelius was bustling about, and Callan sat by his wife's bedside, dark circles far lighter than they had been the day before. Dani wondered if someone had drugged him to sleep with a potion.

The second he saw them, Callan jumped up and crushed them with a hug.

"I'm so relieved that you two are back. I've been worried sick."

Dani had been expecting a lot more scolding first. Maybe he was just in a better mood after resting.

"We're sorry we left like that, but we were able to get the root that can save Mom, and you should focus on that first." Will spoke so fast that Callan couldn't have gotten a word in if he wanted to.

"Do you have it?" Cornelius asked.

Will eagerly handed it over.

"Good. I've had to give smaller doses to hold out. We almost sent a search party."

Dani smiled uneasily. "A search party? Anders and Libby were with us."

"Yes, and they are very capable, but even we bang to lose hope of your return," Edon said, walking in with Giselle, Grennet, Arabella, and Cordelia.

"We were gone only a day." Will was just as confused as Dani felt.

"You both have been gone for over a week." Giselle exchanged a worried glance with Grennet.

"A week!" Dani and Will were so loud it was impossible to tell which voice was which.

Dani recovered first. "Mom. How is she … Is she okay?"

“That’s why I’ve been rationing. She’s fine, but I’m going to get to work with this.” Cornelius held up the root and walked out.

“We were gone for less than a day, I don’t understand.” Will shook his head so hard Dani expected it to fall off.

“It’s the Forest,” Dani swallowed. “That’s probably one of the traps.”

The Magicals nodded.

“We didn’t know we were gone that long,” Will apologized.

Callan nodded. “I know, but I will scold and possibly punish you both later for how dangerous that choice was. For now, I need to stay with your mother, and you two should go get ready.”

“Ready for what?” Dani beat her brother to the question.

“The Lirelight.” Iris stepped into the room, not even hiding her satisfaction that she knew something they didn’t. “It’s tonight.”

CHAPTER THIRTY-SIX

Dani stood at the top of the staircase, wishing that she could run far, far away … or at least change out of her heels.

The Magicals hadn't allowed her to wait for her mother to recover, so Dani had been forced to return to her bedroom and prepare for the most important night of her life.

Their words, not hers.

Libby had taken charge immediately, shooing everyone else out to allow Dani a second to breathe before laying out the monstrosity of a dress that had been picked out and getting the jewelry ready.

Dani had threatened to not leave her bedroom if Libby went with an updo, so instead, she did spiral curls in a half-up half-down style. Dani's usual tiara had been replaced with a larger one even more studded with pearls and diamonds. It was heavier, more extravagant, and Dani was pretty sure it contained half of the crown jewels.

It required absolute perfect posture to not break her neck, and making it from her bedroom to the stairs without pulling out one of the gazillion pins stuck into her head to keep the tiara in place was already *Mission Impossible Part Two*.

"Well, don't you look handsome." Dani couldn't help but grin when Will joined her, looking every bit the Crown Prince and equally as uncomfortable in his attire.

"Well, don't you look sparkly," he shot back, helping her down the stairs. "Nice dress."

Dani rolled her eyes. "Thanks."

The gown was silver, off the shoulder, and very, very large. The skirt and bodice were adorned with diamonds and pearls, much like her tiara, but the skirt itself was at least thirty layers of embellished tulle that made tripping unbelievably easy. In addition, Libby had chosen a choker and pearl earrings, making movement of any kind difficult.

"How much time do you give it before our friends tease us?" Will fiddled with his sleeves, embellished and surely itchy as they reached the foyer.

Dani shrugged. "How fast can Amery get to us?"

Will shuddered. "Good point."

The ballroom was packed with guests, most of them noble, some teenagers and some adults. The Magicals had been holding court since the guests had arrived just like any other ball. The only difference was that this time, every single brytlyn was there to celebrate the twins, despite the fact that the guests of honor were not yet fourteen.

The Magicals had answered that concern with the simple answer of the realm needing something to celebrate, and the close birthday of the Stallards was perfect. Dani and Will had both been mostly relieved about the lack of preparation they had to do, but it was still overwhelming to be thrown in with no notice.

"Oh, no." Dani covered her face with her hands, nearly getting mascara on her gloves as they turned into the ballroom entrance.

"Oh, yes," Everett and Lydia said together, waiting by the doors.

"This is not fair," Will groaned, squeezing his eyes shut as if he could pretend it wasn't happening.

"Trust us, we are just as forced into this as you two are," Lydia promised, smoothing a wrinkle in her gown.

Everett sullenly nodded. "Our parents have had this worked out for months now, I guess. Callan and Amandine figured that you two wouldn't want to pick anyone, so they picked for you."

"We have no choice, do we?" Dani was well aware that if they tried to hide, someone would be sent to find them. Grantham was right inside the door, and the Magicals would not hesitate to search the castle.

"Not unless you want us to be grounded for eternity," Everett griped miserably.

Dani twisted her gloves, silver to match the rest of her ensemble. "Your parents weren't too harsh on you, were they?"

"They were just glad that we all came back alive. Though they did say that perhaps Amery and I weren't the bad influences they assumed," Lydia admitted.

"You and Amery are bad influences on us?" Will lifted a skeptical brow.

She shrugged. "They seemed to think so, considering our strong personalities."

"My parents said mostly the same. Though it was implied that if I didn't escort you, I wouldn't be able to leave Umbergrove for a month."

"Favian?" Will guessed.

"Genevieve." Dani knew better.

Everett nodded. "Mom figured it was a worthy threat. Here I am."

"We just need to walk into the ballroom and stick together. Not just the four of us, but Eldridge and Amery too. No one can force us to dance if we don't split up."

"It isn't the worst plan we've ever had," Will concluded.

"Dad isn't even coming. He's staying with Mom just in case Cornelius can produce a miracle."

Lydia paused for a moment before agreeing. "Hopefully, no one will care that we don't feel very much like dancing for them."

"Our mother is still dying. They shouldn't care." Dani hoped they wouldn't, at least.

"The Magicals will," Everett warned.

"Then we avoid them at all costs."

"That does sound fun," Lydia considered.

"Are you four ready?" Grantham exited the ballroom, shutting the door quickly behind him.

"Not even close." Dani put a smile on her face and took Everett's arm.

"If my twin does anything stupid, feel free to punch him. I don't mind." Lydia did the same with Will, looking perfectly in place with her rose-colored gown that swirled as she stepped forward.

"What's the plan if we see anyone we know?" Dani asked.

"Oh, she's got a point. A good chunk of our grade is here."

"More than usual?" Many of their classmates at Crystalium came from nobility too and attended events frequently.

"More than half at minimum."

"Smile and wave?"

"And pretend we don't recognize them at all. Perfect plan."

"It's something, at least."

"You will all be fine." Grantham said the words less to reassure the kids and more to actually get them inside, but the result was the same. Dani and Will were welcomed into a sea of people with Everett and Lydia beside them. There was a lot of clapping and noise in general until the four of them met the Magicals in the center of the room.

Dani wasn't paying attention for most of the speech, but from the parts that she did hear, it was essentially the Magicals praising them for their leadership, talent, and powers—Speed and Transferer only—and just overall telling the assembled masses how proud they and the King and Queen were of the Stallards.

It ended with more clapping and some whooping that suspiciously sounded like a certain Varron and Callisto, and as soon as they could, the four of them booked it to the side. Anders met them there with Leo, who, for a bodyguard who hadn't seen his charge in a week, was pretty mild, greeting Will with only a pat on the shoulder.

"You did well up there," Anders told Dani, who was very busy trying to stop her tiara from digging into her skull. "Very regal."

She gritted her teeth together in a pained smile. "Thanks. My head is pounding."

"How heavy is that thing?" Everett asked.

"Too heavy," Dani muttered.

"Don't you dare mess up your hair." Libby rushed over, already giving Dani a warning look.

Dani didn't let go of her tiara. "My head is throbbing!"

"Beauty is pain."

"Can I just take one pin out?" Dani pleaded.

Lydia stared her down. "Absolutely not. That would ruin the look."

Dani ignored her. "No one is going to notice one pin missing."

"Lydia has just as many, and I don't see her complaining." Libby pulled her hand away and put the pin back in, much to her charge's dismay.

Lydia gave a sympathetic smile. "I'm using jeweled barrettes; they don't hurt as much."

"So, they aren't digging into your scalp?"

"Nope, though I'm very sorry that they're digging into yours."

Dani nodded graciously. "Thank you."

"Is anyone looking at us right now?" Will asked, ignoring the complaints Dani was frantically whispering to Libby.

"Not at the moment," Anders answered, fully turning away.

"Good. Anyone want to get dessert with me?"

"I'll go!" Everett offered.

"Want to come?" Lydia asked Dani.

She shook her aching head. "I'm okay. I think I might stay here for a second."

Lydia shrugged. "Okay. Do you want anything, then?"

"I'll take something!" Amery walked up before the three could leave. "Did you hear us cheering, by the way? I told Eld to be as loud as possible."

"We heard," Dani said.

"We all heard," Libby corrected.

Amery clapped his hands, applauding himself for a job well done. "Good; then it worked. You all look very nice, by the way, especially for brytlyns who were attacked this morning."

"Technically, it wasn't this morning," Will pointed out.

"You called it," Lydia told Dani. "You said everything was a trap, and you were right."

"Maybe that was the point?" Everett offered. "If the time part is a trap, then maybe the danger was supposed to make us want to stay or at least feel comfortable doing so."

"And then some brytlyns never leave. Pretty solid tactic, I suppose." Amery whistled.

"It's genius. Terrifying but genius," Dani commended.

"At least we got out," Will commented.

"And I didn't have to be king." Amery shuddered at the memory.

"I don't think we can sneak out of this ball," Lydia decided, subtly directing everyone's gaze to the crowd, where, sure enough, more than a few pairs of eyes were watching.

"As much as I'd love to go to Frovland, I don't think that it's even smart to try." Dani knew how much panic would be caused if they vanished again. Not to mention the punishments.

"As much as I wish I didn't, I agree. Please get me a fudge cake," Amery said somberly.

"Of course," Will promised and then they took off, leaving Dani with her self-proclaimed sidekick. Anders and Libby had already dispersed into the crowd.

"Do you think this is weird?" Amery asked the question so softly that Dani almost didn't hear it.

"What?"

"We get back from a forest stuck in time, and now we're at a Lirelight you didn't even know was planned."

"It's weird," she agreed. "My mom isn't even healed, and Will and I are being used to make everyone feel better about it."

"It's not fair," Amery affirmed.

Dani snorted. "Exactly."

"The Magicals are supposed to put the entire family first. I think sometimes they forget that you are included in that."

"It's not all of them," Dani defended.

Amery stayed unconvinced. "Giselle and Grennet could do more to help you."

"Decisions require a majority, Amery."

"I know," he said. "But have you ever thought that the reason you hate your powers so much is because every time you do something, the Magicals make it out to be something bigger?"

Dani despised admitting that Amery was right about anything, especially when they both knew it.

She cleared her throat, hoping her voice would come out strong. "Their job is to keep the realm safe from all threats."

"Not from you. You know that, right?" Amery's face creased with worry.

Dani averted her eyes. "If I say yes, will you not give me a pep talk?"

"If you say yes, I'm going to know that you're lying, but out of the kindness of my heart, I will escort you around the room because you'd prefer that to the alternative." Amery pointed to the side, and Dani had to fix her face into a smile.

Iris was walking straight toward her. And that was never good.

"Come on, Mystery." Amery grabbed her hand and tugged her away, traitorously bringing them closer to the dancing.

"You cannot be serious." Dani wasn't sure if she wanted to laugh or glare at him.

Amery grinned. "One dance and the Magicals will be off your back, and we can go tackle the dessert table."

 "I don't know if I can actually eat anything in this dress."

"If I have learned anything about you, it's that you always have room for fudge cakes."

"That's true," Dani agreed. "One dance, and then treats. Deal?"

"You have a deal."

And so Dani let Amery lead her to the center of the ballroom.

CHAPTER THIRTY-SEVEN

Dani wasn't a fan of dancing for many, many reasons.

It was formal, embarrassing, and pretty difficult for something that all members of brytlyn nobility were supposed to know from birth.

Dancing with Amery was the exact opposite. He turned it into a game within two steps, deciding to guess what power each guest around them had while supplying them with ridiculous names.

"See, that one is named Grimhilda, and she has a lovely hobby of shooting spheres of light at people," Amery announced, looking over Dani's shoulder at a brytlyn in a green gown.

"I'll take your word for it." Dani couldn't crane her neck far enough to get a good glimpse until they turned. "Grimhilda?"

"It's a good name," Amery promised, twirling her.

Dani smiled wryly. "I've never met anyone with that name. Ever."

"Clearly, brytlyns these days don't have my incredible naming skills, then. What a shame."

"Clearly." Dani snorted. Amery was taller than her, but not by that much, which made dancing a lot easier. He knew exactly what he was doing and made just enough jokes to make the whole thing not awkward, which she greatly appreciated.

Dani was secretly glad that he was dancing with her instead of Everett. For reasons she still didn't understand, she felt comfortable with Amery, far more than she felt with the Callisto boys, both of whom were some of her closest friends.

Amery made her laugh. Sometimes, that was better than having someone share in her worries.

"Okay, guy in the purple jacket. Flame, Geronimo."

"Geronimo?"

"Don't insult my pick!"

"Well, you started it," Amery said. "But you did get one point, Mystery. Lord Carnegie is a flame."

Dani grinned. "So, I'm a genius."

"You're a good guesser, that's all," Amery corrected.

"And you're a sore loser."

"A sore loser who saved you from your arch nemesis," Amery said, smirking triumphantly.

"I didn't need saving!"

"Of course not. But it's the least that I could do for my fearless leader."

Dani rolled her eyes. "I'm the farthest thing."

"Yet you led us to a forest of doom and insisted upon fighting the rebels trying to kill you?" Amery bragged on her behalf.

"I didn't want anything to happen to you guys, so I fought back," Dani explained. "Ivy was our leader for the trip anyway."

"We wouldn't have gone if it wasn't for you. You inspire people."

"I have really amazing friends. There's a difference."

Amery scoffed. "As much as I usually love getting compliments, especially from you, our little band of thieves is hardly amazing. Joining The Golden Eagle didn't happen because of us, helping the realm didn't happen because of us, and keeping your mom alive didn't happen because of us."

"You all helped a lot," Dani argued.

"I can't speak for my sister or your brother and the Callistos, but I know that before I met you, I wouldn't have ever done anything like this."

Dani let him twirl her, listening patiently.

"When we were younger, Will and I were closer than he was with the Callistos. He was sheltered and sick of having to be perfect all the time; I had a knack for fun and adventure. We were the best of buds in no time at all."

Dani had known that her brother had grown up with the Callisto boys and Varron twins, but she hadn't known the exact specifics.

"When we were all together, I knew that I needed to somehow be different, and since Everett—at least, at that point—was more mature than most, I knew I was to be the loose cannon of the group. The laid back, bad influence with just enough noble upbringing to have spectacular manners."

Dani wasn't used to Amery being so open with her, his usual

confidence stripped away as they danced. She liked that he felt like he could be honest with her like she was honest with him.

"That must've been hard." Changing to fit in always seemed to be.

Amery laughed bitterly. "Over time, it became more natural, not that it was a lie either. That's why I think becoming friends with you is a good thing. I can be something else, be a part of something good."

"You are a good person, Amery Varron. Don't ever doubt that."

"And you, Dani Stallard, are the most incredible brytlyn that I have ever met."

And then the perfect moment ended.

Flames appeared to drop from the ceiling, spraying sparks everywhere.

Guests ran. Glass shattered. Brytlyns screamed. Amery pushed Dani behind him.

It took a moment for Dani to process the chaos going on around her, but as soon as she did, she pulled her gloves off and prepared to let her sparks go wild.

Bartholomew was here.

Behind him were twenty more members of The Midnight Dragon.

CHAPTER THIRTY-EIGHT

Anders made it to their side in seconds, hauling both Dani and Amery to the side of the ballroom, sword raised.

"Libby is with your siblings and friends," he said, his face a mask of calm.

"Good," Amery said.

Dani almost reached for Amery's hand but stopped herself. Her gloves were being trampled by the guests rushing out of the ballroom. "She should get them out."

"I am sure that she will," Anders promised.

"You need to leave too," Dani ordered Amery.

"I'm not going anywhere." He shook his head and sped off, returning in barely twenty seconds with a sword.

Anders narrowed his eyes. "This is not a good idea."

"Come out, come out, little hero!" Bartholomew called, forcing Anders to pull them deeper into a corner blocked off by curtains. "If you surrender in peace, no one has to get hurt."

"You need to leave now, Amery." Dani felt her hands shaking, a million thoughts and plans flooding her brain as the Magicals made their way forward along with hundreds of guards, filling the room.

"We're a team. We fight as a team." Amery was determined, his confidence not even wavering for a second. "Besides, I know how to use this, and you shouldn't have to do this alone."

"I agree with my brother," Lydia said, leading the rest of their makeshift team to the corner.

"Where is Libby?" Anders demanded, keeping one eye on the crowd.

Eldridge pointed to the second line of guards. "Somewhere up there. She told us to meet up with you."

Anders gritted his teeth so loud that Dani expected them to be ground to dust. "They want Dani. They don't care how they get her, but they want her. I need you six to blink away from here. Go somewhere safe."

"If we can get upstairs, we can grab a medallion, go to Frovland," Everett suggested.

Dani tugged on her fingers. "They're taking over, just like the prophecy said. They'll win either way, regardless of if I leave."

"I don't plan on making it easy for them," Anders vowed, and Dani wasn't sure if it made her feel better or worse that he wasn't saying that they would win.

Bartholomew seemed to have gotten bored of whatever the Magicals were trying to negotiate, and he carelessly knocked a line of guards back and sent the others running.

"I know the Savior is here somewhere!" Dani shrunk further into the curtains, her vision blurring with tears of terror. Lydia made it to her first, the boys forming a human shield around her right after.

"She is not." Iris, to the immense shock of Dani's entire group, was the one who spoke up.

"Our leader informed us that this party was in her honor." Bartholomew evidently was a flame and very proud of that fact, heaving a great ball of fire at the Magicals.

Dani peeked out of the curtain's edge, breathing a sigh of relief when they all managed to escape and not be set on fire. Even Iris.

"Go upstairs. She may have fled in the chaos," he ordered once the Magicals had scattered. "At the very least, you can get to her parents. The Queen has not yet recovered."

Dani felt her hands shake, raw power surging just as Anders whispered something to Will, and the group sprinted away. To where, she wasn't sure. She swiped the tears off her cheeks frantically, rushing away from the curtain before she lost the shred of hope stirring her on.

"I'm right here!" She threw her arms out wide and walked forward, shooting sparks at the guards about to leave, forcing them away from the danger. Anders tried to force her behind him again, but she blasted him back, knocking him unconscious. She took out Libby with the same when she ran over, reminding herself that it was only to keep them safe.

Bartholomew only smiled pleasantly. "I apologize for the intrusion, Dani. Should I be offering my congratulations for this event?"

Bartholomew had a sphere of flames above his palm, and Dani had sparks above hers.

"Probably." Dani cleared the thickness from her throat. "I'd accept you leaving and never coming back as my gift."

"The leader would not accept that, I'm afraid." He shrugged

carelessly.

Dani glared. "So, you want to battle me again? You lost."

"Yes, I recall. Since you asked, no, I don't want another fight. I simply need you out of the picture so that our leader can continue her mission."

Dani shook her head in disgust. "I'm really not a fan of your leader,"

Bartholomew shook his head mournfully. "That's a shame. She truly holds you in high regard."

"Well, then, why isn't she here herself?"

"She is quite busy at the moment. Many things were put on hold to find out when the Lirelight was going to take place."

"To be fair, I didn't know until I had to get ready," Dani said, hoping she sounded unbothered instead of terrified.

"Yes, yes. Your father made the decision after you returned to save your dying mother. Another shame that your physician still hasn't been able to figure out what is wrong with her."

Dani swallowed thickly. "How did you know about that?"

"Because I told him." Giselle smiled, a cruel, nasty smile that looked foreign on her face. She wore a cloak on top of her lilac gown, a blue one with a flame.

"You?" Dani felt tears sting her eyes, but she refused to let them drop, allowing the sparks in her hand to multiply instead.

She sneered. "You didn't think I was your favorite advisor for a reason, did you?"

Dani curled her other hand into a fist to stop it from shaking. "You're the traitor."

"Score one for the princess," Giselle declared, voice full of sarcasm. "Now, Bartholomew, I have a job for you. Wilfred, Amery, Lydia, Everett, and Eldridge are around here somewhere. Find them and bring them to me."

"Yes, ma'am."

Giselle nodded curtly, turning to her waiting operatives. "And Anders and Libby need to be restrained immediately."

"Not a problem, ma'am. As you wish, ma'am."

Dani didn't even let them take two steps.

She took down the operatives deployed to get her friends with the sparks above her left hand and the ones about to take her guards with the sparks she formed above her right. The blasts were strong enough to knock them fully out, and Dani didn't even flinch. Besides, it felt good to knock Bartholomew and his oily smile out too.

A spark sphere came naturally, but Dani refused to let it form. If she wanted to conserve her power enough to make it out alive, then she couldn't risk it.

Giselle clapped. "Well, I see that you've been improving nicely. There was never really any doubt about that; you are quite a fast learner."

"Why are you doing this?" Dani's voice came out shaky and raw as if she'd been screaming for hours.

"Because the realm has been in tatters for a very long time, and the people who are in charge are doing nothing to fix it."

"My parents are doing a fantastic job. You're only doing this because a prophecy said that it would happen again."

"The ideals of our predecessors were correct, and we are going to follow through with them," Giselle stated plainly, looking positively bored with having to deal with a teenager on the verge of a breakdown.

"I trusted you. We all trusted you!" A wave of sparks flew around the room like shooting stars, aimed straight for Giselle.

She sidestepped casually. "A terrible choice, really. Though being a Magical did provide a very good opportunity to watch over you, make sure that my organization had all the intel that they needed."

"Your organization … You're the leader too."

"Dani, you really are a clever girl. Always have been. Unfortunately, you failed when it mattered most."

"What does that mean?" Dani poised another sphere of sparks in both hands, ready to strike.

"You never questioned why Callan insisted upon the Lirelight tonight—mistake number one of the great and powerful chosen one. Transferers can transfer thoughts, as I know I've explained to you, but they can also change thoughts if they are skilled enough."

"You are." Dani seethed.

"I am. Just like I'm skilled enough to slip a very powerful but completely untraceable and odorless poison into your mother's tea during a meeting. She always thought that I was one of the best advisors, loyal, intelligent, good with kids. You and Amandine are very similar."

"Yes, we are." Dani stood straighter, trying to collect herself. "And you're nothing but a pathetic, power-hungry loser."

Giselle inclined a perfectly arched brow. "That's the best you can come up with? I thought Amery had taught you better than that."

"Don't you dare bring him into this," Dani fumed, her sparks shooting up around her.

"Touchy, touchy. Someone clearly is having a bad day"

"Says the woman whose operatives have been taken down by a thirteen-year-old who didn't know magic existed until a few months ago."

"I forget how overconfident you teenagers can be. Your father wasn't the only one I was able to use my power on. The castle inhabitants, except for your two unconscious protectors, band of adorable little thieves, and your lovely parents, of course, are more or less under my control."

Dani shrugged, attempting to look half as confident as Lydia did every day of her life. "Bring it on. I think I can handle a few brytlyns."

"Just the answer I was looking for." Giselle offered another insincere smile, stretching her arms majestically as guards that had run out in fear not long before charged back in, settling around Dani. The rest of the Magicals followed suit, their eyes flashing purple.

The guards poised their swords at her as if in battle against a foreign army.

Dani called more sparks, ready to create a spark sphere to protect herself if needed. That was what she'd been trained to do, and deviating from her instructions now felt like a really bad tactical decision.

She had only a second to take one last shaky breath.

And then they charged.

CHAPTER THIRTY-NINE

Dani thought that she was holding her own for someone being attacked and outrageously outnumbered.

She decided against the spark sphere to get a better view of the number of brytlyns trying to charge at her. The Magicals were hanging back, letting the hundreds of guards surround her on all sides.

The guards were all in sync with each other, mindless zombies under the same command. Dani recognized most of them. They had been kind to her.

Now, they were trying to stab her.

Dani was forced into a different approach. Bursts of red electricity were forming around her in a loose spark sphere, whipping fast enough to ward off swords while spirals of tentacle-like sparks fought offense.

She stretched a hand out, forcing one tentacle all the way to Giselle. Sparks coiled around her too, flickers of light surrounding the entire ballroom. It would have been an exquisite sight if not for the strain being put on the wielder and the amount of damage she was allowing herself to create. Brytlyns were dropping like flies, swarmed by sparks pulsing out in an endless cycle.

The voice in the back of her mind was telling Dani to be careful, not to overdo it and lose control. She couldn't. But she was also angry at Giselle, replaying every single memory, looking for every single sign. Giselle had been there to tell Dani the truth about her life, the one who brought her to Breckindale, the one who gave her the scroll to find The Golden Eagle.

Dani felt sick.

The Magical she'd trusted most had been the one conducting her downfall.

Her power surged, growing stronger and faster as Dani's emotions spiraled, growing and growing until the room was covered floor to ceiling.

And then she lost it. The ground and the sky and where and who she was.
The magic consumed her, folding in on itself until the protective shell of sparks deserted its owner.

"Get her!" Giselle ordered.

Dani curled herself into a ball, tears staining her pasty white cheeks. They forced her into a standing position, weakly getting pushed by the princess.

Her vision dissolved into colorful blotches, but eventually, the dizziness subsided, though she was immediately regretful when her senses sharpened.

One guard had his sword pressed against her throat with zero qualms about letting her go.

Another forced gloves onto her hands, thick ones that felt strangely metallic.

"What are these?" Dani gritted out.

"Specially made gloves. They lock once they're on you and are very, very difficult to take off. Your powers, both of them, are null and void."

Dani's brain felt hazy, but she had enough consciousness to glare at Giselle with everything she had, just not enough to figure out a way out.

Fortunately, she didn't have to. Will's voice passed through her head, near perfect transference.

Hang on. Ivy and Eagle operatives are about to come in and get you out. Be ready in five.

Five?

She really hoped her brother didn't mean five minutes.

Her answer came in the form of poignant smoke and an angry dragon.

Before the guards or Giselle could move, the room was swarmed by golden cloaks, weapons and powers at the ready.

"Get Anders and Libby, Ember!" Dani struggled against the operatives holding her, but they didn't budge. "Hurry!"

Ember made a sound that seemed to be as close to a battle cry as a dragon could muster, shaking off and knocking down a good number of enemies with her wings as she raced to grab Libby.

Ivy and four others made it to Dani first. Ivy wielded two swords, both with deadly aim at the operatives keeping her charge captive.

"Two options." Ivy managed to look just as intimidating with a pleasant expression as she did with a glare. "Give me the girl, or be impaled by my sword. Your choice."

The guards didn't speak, but they didn't move either. Dani wondered if they really were mindless zombies, incapable of performing actions Giselle didn't command.

"Too bad, then." With the kind of grace Dani only wished for, Ivy did some sort of ninja scissor spin kick, knocking away the sword poised to rip into Dani's throat. Her companions attacked the operatives, knocking them down.

Ivy, uncharacteristically gentle, grabbed Dani's arm and tugged her to her side. "Do they hurt?" she asked, glancing down at the gloves.

Dani nodded, trying to get a glimpse of the action. "I knocked Anders out."

"Smart. He would've hurt himself defending you. He'll be fine; Ember has him." Ivy pointed to where Ember had heaved Libby onto her back and was holding Anders by his armor. To the dragon, she said, "Go ahead, Ember. I've got her. We'll meet soon."

"Meet where?" Dani doubted going to Frovland was safe at the moment.

"You'll see." Ivy shrugged off a satchel she was carrying and handed it to Dani. "Longlive is in there; you'll need it."

"Thanks." Dani reached inside the bag and fished her sword out, immediately feeling better. "What's the plan?"

"We're leaving. Now."

"What about Giselle? What about my parents?"

"Everything will be taken care of. Right now, I have to get you to safety."

Dani shook her head. "We can't just leave. They'll overrun it."

"And you'll take it back," Ivy promised, practically pushing her behind a group of their operatives. "Now, we may have to fight our way out. How comfortable do you feel with using your sword as opposed to magic?"

Dani held up her gloved hands. "It's the only option."

"You should be fine."

Dani didn't find the comment very reassuring, but Ivy probably hadn't meant it as such anyway. "What way?"

"The front has been cleared. That's how I got in and got your friends out. They just left, I believe."

"Are they meeting us too?"

Ivy nodded. "Should already be there now if they listened. Never fall."

"Never fall," Dani echoed, following Ivy out of the ballroom and around to the main foyer. It was relatively empty, but the front doors were still guarded.

Dani raised Longlive like she'd done it a thousand times. When she charged, it felt like the lie had a glimmer of truth to it.

The sword gave her a rush of power and seemed to have a mind of its own, leading Dani in all the right positions to avoid the swords her enemies skillfully wielded against her.

Ivy was faster and a lot less hesitant to cause harm. Within another minute, the remaining guards had dropped, and Dani was hurrying to get outside behind her protector.

"Grab on," Ivy instructed, holding a silver medallion with a black stone in the center. Dani had only latched onto her hand for a second before they disappeared.

The blink was rocky, and Dani felt queasy when she landed.

"Where are we?" They were in some sort of field, standing in front of a tall, grassy hill.

"Sleetvault, The Golden Eagle's base in a realm called Elomarsh. It's the farthest realm from Breckindale," Ivy explained.

"Is that why you chose it?" Dani asked.

"I didn't choose it; your council did. In case they ever tried to take you or do harm, my job was to get you all here safely and act as a guard."

"Where is it?"

Ivy pointed at the hill. A door opened from the center of it, and Will and Lydia peeked out. Both looked wary but relatively unharmed.

"Are Anders and Libby going to be okay?" Dani questioned.

Ivy nodded. "They'll be fine. You just knocked them out pretty good. Other than that, they are perfectly unharmed."

Dani almost smiled, relieved that, at the very least, her friends were okay. "How long are we staying here?"

Ivy paused as if she was considering what to say. Finally, she took a breath. "Until you are ready to end this."

Dani pretended her sword was the most interesting thing in the realm. She knew that eventually, Gernon Cryter would be proven correct.

She'd never expected it to happen like this.

"It's begun, hasn't it?"

Ivy nodded, confirming Dani's worst fears and also, in a strange way, her relief.

The prophecy was coming true.